£4 99

Homu

CU00922844

ALEKSANDAR PROKOPIEV

HOMUNCULUS

FAIRY TALES FROM THE LEFT POCKET

Translated from the Macedonian by Will Firth

istrosbooks

English language edition first published by
Istros Books
London, United Kingdom www.istrosbooks.com

First published in Macedonian as *Човечулец: бајки од левиот џеб*,
Magor, Skopje 2011
The second story, *'Snakelet'*, was first published in Best European Fiction
2015, Dalkey Archive Press, Champaign/Dublin/London, 2014

© Aleksandar Prokopiev, 2015

The right of Aleksandar Prokopiev to be identified as the author of this work has
been asserted in accordance with the Copyright, Designs and Patents Act, 1988

Translation © Will Firth, 2015
Foreword © Fiona Sampson, 2015

Edited by S.D. Curtis

Cover design & typesetting: Davor Pukljak, www.frontispis.hr

ISBN: 978-1-908236-23-4

Printed in England by
CMP (UK), Poole, Dorset www.cmp-up.com

Education and Culture DG

Culture Programme

This project has been funded with support from the European Commission. This
publication reflects the views only of the author, and the Commission cannot be held
responsible for any use which may be made of the information contained therein.

Foreword

Aleksandar Prokopiev's fiction resembles very little that will be familiar to English readers. It has the fantastical darkness of folk material but, like the novels of Angela Carter, it inflects this matter with high cultural allusions. Tom Thumb rubs shoulders with the humanist philosopher Pico della Mirandola; an icon painter with a talking frog. At the same time, and rather more like the Latin American novelist Roberto Bolaño, Prokopiev creates a fictional world that doesn't differentiate between the invented, the factual and the autobiographical. Much of 'Once Upon a Prokopiev', the last story in this volume, for example, is taken from the writer's own life.

This mixture is exciting and kaleidoscopic. It makes the stories in Homunculus feel hyper-animated, if not hyperbolic. It also has a serious purpose, which is to destabilize the reader, who will no longer be able to keep "the real world" and "fiction" safely apart. In other words, "true" fiction reminds us that our inner lives are composed not only of daydream but also of memory, and – perhaps more sinisterly – not only of truth but of invention. Prokopiev's first collection of short stories, published in 1983, appeared to acknowledge this with its challenging title, *The Young Master of the Game*. And he is indeed a game-playing writer, who is not merely playful but uses codes and sophisticated rules to create narratives layered with meanings.

Some of this playfulness comes directly from folk material, whose dream logic and incompletion literary writers have long found evocative but which this author deploys with real knowledge. Prokopiev's doctoral work, undertaken at the University of Belgrade and the Sorbonne, conducted original research into the folk stories of what was then southern Yugoslavia. An early collection of essays is titled *Fairy-story On the Road* (1996), and he is now the Professor of Comparative Literature at the National University of Ss Cyril and Methodius.

Nevertheless, Prokopiev would describe himself as a postmodernist, an orientation that other titles among his thirteen collections of fiction and essays suggest. These include ...*or...* (1986), *Anti-instructions for Personal Use* (2000) and *Postmodern Babylon* (2000). But there's nothing po-faced or overly systemic about this engagement with philosophy. Prokopiev is always fun to read. In fact, in his native Macedonia, this former rock star – he was a founder member of the New Wave band Idoli, notorious for their ambiguous anthem 'I seldom see you with girls' – is something of a media don, as well as a highly influential cultural critic. In that southernmost state of the old "Southern Slavs" – *yugo* means south – the rural and the urban, tradition and the contemporary world, are closer neighbours than they are in many northern European countries. An intellectual like Prokopiev, who was born in the capital, Skopje, in 1953, isn't divorced from the world of Roma music, peasant farming and rural superstition that still surrounds and intermingles with the more globalized culture of university or city bar.

For much of the year, the people of Skopje and its hinterland lead an outdoor, public life of terraces and cafes. This is also a post-communist culture, and those who grew up here before 1989 – as Prokopiev did – became accustomed to relatively little personal space. This gives the Republic's culture, like that of its Balkan neighbours an oral vibrancy, which Prokopiev brilliantly and continually captures. One small example: when the swan-girl's breasts, in 'The Man with One Wing', start out 'orange-shaped' but soon grow 'grapefruit-shaped', our narrator is making a little play on the mounting hyperbole of traditional story-telling.

For Prokopiev is a storyteller, not a textual mechanic. His *contes* are full of emotion, and of archetype. They are also full of darkness, as befits a country still sitting on the fault line that produced the wars, which pulled the former Yugoslavia apart at the end of the twentieth century. The war in Macedonia was the last to be formally concluded; nevertheless, this small country of just over two million inhabitants did not allow itself to be torn apart along ethnic or religious grounds. It remains a mixed Orthodox Christian and Muslim country, whose official languages are Macedonian – a Slav language closely related to Bulgarian which uses the Cyrillic alphabet – and, in municipalities with a local majority population, Albanian, an Indo-European language which has no relatives but uses the Roman alphabet.

There is tremendous intimacy in writing for a language-community of roughly one and a half million people. Aleksandar Prokopiev is by turns mischievous – in 'The Dance of the Coloured Handkerchiefs', a story to make boys and girls of all ages smile, the protagonist-handkerchief longs for snot – admonitory. 'Marko's Little Sister' reads like a cross between 'The Boy who Cried Wolf' and an Awful Warning against self-harm) and is challenging: "The smell of the forest, the smell of gunpowder, and the calm certainty of death. How exciting it is!" ends 'The Huntsman'. But, however much the intimate raconteur appeals to our inner child, much more is also going on in such fictions. The shadows these bedside stories cast are genuine monsters, as in this volume's parables about morality, ('Neverland', 'The Huntsman'), history ('Human, All Too Human', 'The Haji, The Shoemaker and the Fool'), and identity ('A Christmas Tale', 'Homunculus').

That Prokopiev manages to combine the great and the small, coining archetypes while winking at a local joke over a glass of Skopsko beer, is both astonishing and delightful. Now perhaps the 'middle-aged master of the game', he is unique in dedicating his writing life almost completely to the short story form. (As well as his essays, a novel, *Peeper*, appeared in 2007 – and was the national entry for the Balkanika Prize.) The results can be seen in his influence on many middle-generation Balkan writers, and in the numerous foreign editions, and the awards, his work has received: culminating in the international Balkanika Prize 2010, awarded to *Homunculus*.

Often surreal, sometimes inexplicable, Aleksandar Prokopiev is one of the 'must-reads'. He is a teasing, telling interlocutor who likes to play the naïve; the brilliant Fool who is a figure as recognizable from our traditions as from his own. These shape-shifting stories remain adamantly and radically open for us to interpret.

They challenge us to accept, even to embrace, our own confusion: implying, perhaps, that life itself is as confusing as any fable. To read them is to glimpse the wildness at the heart of Europe.

FIONA SAMPSON

Coleshill 24/2/15

Contents

*This fairy tale is to be told in the morning while eating
a fry-up for breakfast after a night's heavy drinking*

Tom Thumb

Have you got back together with that fellow who's the same age as me, Mum? Oh, if only I weren't your son... It's not that I've got anything against him. He's a good man, and he paid the 714 euros for my treatment. I'd like to take this opportunity to thank him for thinking of me and paying for my stay at the sanatorium, although it did look more like some kind of corrective institution than a place where people are cured. You know what I mean. Soon after I got there, during the first week of my stay, I was punished for listening to music during the so-called 'hours of rest' between 3pm and 5.30pm. How could I have known that the music from my iPad would be a nuisance to anyone? But I was caught. And she – Kyrie the Matron – ordered that I be locked up for two whole days and nights in an empty cellar where a chair riveted to the floor was the only furniture. I was tied to that chair and an unbearably strong spotlight was set up to shine straight in my face. You can imagine how I felt, Mum, with that sharp needle of light piercing the pupils of my eyes and the tight rope cutting into my body. I was so distressed and helpless there in the 'Damned Cell', as the kids at the sanatorium called that dreadful cellar with no windows and only a slit in the iron door. Within just a few hours you lose track of whether the sun is shining outside or people are sleeping peacefully in the stillness of the night. After a terribly long time, someone opens the hole in the door and peers at you. You can feel their cold, sneering gaze but can't see who it is because your eyes feel like they're covered with blisters of light from the constant aggression of the spotlight. Somewhere out there, beyond that little hole, behind that sarcastic tormentor, there exists a world in which people talk, move about, and sometimes, perhaps, even laugh.

You start to feel that the unpleasant, restricted world of the sanatorium is beautiful and free compared to the 'Damned Cell'. Yes, free! But then you're back in prison with the light stabbing you like an executioner's knife for a long, long time without end... Until you start yelling and screaming like crazy, and that's what you've become. You scream like a wild thing and howl with frayed vocal chords in a voice you've only heard twice before: at your own birth, and that time in the bathroom. They unlock the door. You hear Kyrie the Matron approaching and recognize her step but can't see her in the murderous light. She comes up to you and you know she's observing you with disdain. You can imagine she's wearing black trousers, as usual, and the black coat she always buttons up, neat and orderly, with the blindingly white collar of a freshly ironed shirt showing at the neck. And then you hear her voice.

Mummy, if anyone has cared for me since my birth, it was you, even though I was such a shock to you! You couldn't even admit to yourself that I was your baby. And how could you have? Such a little runt, all covered in black hair as a result of the irritation in your belly. I can imagine how hard it must have been to carry me all through pregnancy, and how much harder when you first saw me – like a wet rat straight out of the sewer. Even the honoured gynaecologist who helped with the delivery, with all respect for your unequalled beauty and the splendour of your vagina gazed in horror when he saw me. And all the more so when he first heard me cry! I know that everyone in the maternity ward was shocked by that horrible noise, which did not sound at all like a baby's voice but much more like the protracted howl of a sick animal. At the time, of course, I was unaware of the terrible effect of my appearance and voice, but ten years later, when puberty took hold of me, I realized I had registered that event in my subconscious, poor me!

I was in the bathroom again, as usual, looking at my face in the mirror and feeling guilty about its appearance. I hated my big nose with its pus-filled pimples, my fat lips with white scabs in the corners – that whole, huge noggin stuck on top of my puny body, like something out of *Punch and Judy*. Only my eyes, which were very bright like those of a ginger tomcat, stared back at me, unpleasantly inhuman and cold even when my body was full of seething anger towards myself. Maybe they were like that because all the difficult experiences I had had since I was a baby had left my eyes dry, without a single tear.

But just when I was standing in front of the mirror facing my ugliness for the umpteenth time, some unknown urge from my rickety chest, some deep sorrow burst out through my carious teeth and escaped as a cry, loud and animal-like, followed by another and yet another, and I began howling there alone in the bathroom, squatting on the floor because I couldn't bear to look at myself any longer. It's lucky you weren't in the flat at the time; you were at a rendezvous with your lover in *Café Journal* and couldn't hear my barbaric cries for help.

Please forgive me, Mummy, for my ugliness! Forgive the worthlessness and putridness of this freak that dares to call itself your son!

Now in the 'Damned Cell', just like in the bathroom, I shed a pool of tears and then started wailing most horribly. Kyrie spoke to me as I was yelling and screaming and blubbering, my face smeared with tears and snot. Her voice was terribly calm: 'Why are you making such a racket?'

'S... sorry... Miss,' I answered, still blinded by the sadistic blade of light and unable to see anything but her dark silhouette.

'How dare you call me Miss!' she interrupted. 'What am I?'

'You're the M... Matron,' I sniffled.

You can imagine how dejected and miserable I felt, Mummy. I tried hard to stop my tears and not make another noise. But I failed; it just wouldn't work. So I wailed for all to hear, and inside as well, and when I was finally able to see her eyes scrutinizing me coldly with no feeling in them other than mastery, I felt so wretched and so punished.

'You deserved your punishment, so now put up with it. And stop that pathetic bawling!' she snarled, as if she could read my mucousy thoughts and was making me feel the full weight of my sentence, now when I was weakest and unable to defend myself.

It was ghastly, but even in that lowliest of positions I cursed Kyrie, that damn bitch. And when she left the cell, still indifferent and harsh, I swore to myself a hundred times over that I would have my revenge. That is the price that tormented souls exact of their tormentors. What else can a midget do – a Quasimodo like me – in the face of the appalling and endless humiliation those such as Kyrie subjected me to in the 'Damned Cell'? Whenever I raised my eyes heavenwards to beg for help, the artificial glare of the spotlight whipped me back to earth, and whenever I tried to heave a sigh, as one small way of relieving my pain, the rope cut deeper into my chest. I know, Mum, that even in such harrowing hours you would be able to shake off evil thoughts and vanquish all misfortune with your inner peace. But I am far from possessing your virtues!

I stuck through the rest of my punishment, the second day and the second night, although I was no longer aware how much time had passed, and when they came in to tell me it was over and untied the blasted rope, I stayed sitting on the chair, withdrawn and dismayed, unable to move a muscle, although the rope had been removed and the door was open. I simply couldn't move, and for a few minutes it felt as if I was blind and deaf – as if I was dead.

Then I pulled myself together, got up from the chair, and walked out of the cell, and even managed a smile. From that day on, I behaved like a model patient, ever obedient, although my spiteful mind was working to devise my revenge.

I will never forget how devotedly you cared for me when I was little – and I must have seemed like a baby for a long time, for I was five times smaller than the other boys my age, more wrinkled and wizened as well, and I didn't grow any bigger. You were torn between your obligations to me and to your lover, it was a real martyrdom, yet you always managed to strike a balance and never gave up despite all the difficulties.

That's why I'm so happy you've found a man who suits you, Mum. Young, capable and virile! Although I have to admit that when you first introduced him to me I felt like taking a bite out of his pretty face. I found him unbearably handsome, with the dark, lively eyes of a dandy, with teeth that shone when he stretched his mouth into a smile, and a charming dimple in his manly chin. I wished

I could savage the seductive symmetry of that face – I wanted to bite deep, draw blood, and butcher that victorious young male's air of superiority. And then his height! That was the end of me, Mother. I had the uncontrollable urge to shorten his long, elegant legs. Not only did I mean him harm but I started plotting straight away how to do it.

With ugly people like me, the spirit is easily corrupted into hatching hellish plans. Our flat is on the fifth floor of a building with no lift. I knew he had the habit of bolting up the stairs on his way to see you and bolting down again after a good lay, like a self-assured billy goat, and I knew he didn't really watch his step. And so one day while he was relishing your voluptuous curves for hours on end – after having first ripped off your black lace knickers, a throwaway learnt from watching too many cheap movies – I set my trap. I stretched a piece of grey string across one of the stairs between the fifth and fourth floors, tying it tightly to the banister on one side and tacking it to the wall on the other. I made sure the string was quite low down (my sort of level!) so he wouldn't notice it.

I know the unpleasant feeling of losing your balance, of your rootless body flying through the air, with your heart beating like mad in fear of what's going to happen when you come down. It only lasts a second or so, but in that short space of time I had the great pleasure of seeing fear change his pretty face into a twisted, bewildered, ugly grimace. He swore, waved his arms in the air and came down on the stairs with a crash. There was a loud crack, like the sound of a thick branch being snapped in half. Then complete silence reigned for a moment as he lay sprawled across the steps, his legs in different directions; he groaned, and his face contorted like in a silent movie as he tried to sit up. But his right leg jutted out sideways, the trouser leg was torn at the knee, and his shin bone stuck out through it, pink and unreal. In that moment of astounding silence my chest filled with a lovely warmth, and then he screamed, and you came bolting down the stairs after him as fast as you could. You dabbed the cheek of his swollen, uglified face with a white handkerchief (loverboy was crying!) and knelt beside him like a good fairy, comforting him with gentle, caring words and constantly kissing him as if he was an injured little bird, not a grown man.

And so I was separated from you again, imprisoned within the walls of my monstrosity. I withdrew into the bathroom, but you didn't even notice I was gone. You were obsessed with your lover's injury, dashing about around him; you called an ambulance and various friends, moved him from the stairs to the bed and pampered him there with devotion, while a whirlwind of jealousy raged inside me despite my best efforts to prevent it. Oh yes, he enjoyed the role of the wounded man, with you there to wait on him day and night, and now he could relish your velvet skin and culinary charms in equal measure. Meanwhile I suffered as the worm of envy gnawed at me and my heart crumbled, but it was all in vain – you were bound to be constantly by his side, and all because of my idiocy!

I know I was a burden to you, Mother, even when I was still in your belly. That Party functionary who enjoyed your magnificent body night after night, my supposed father, shamelessly abandoned you when you told him you were pregnant. He kicked you out without a word, forgetting all the times he had crept between your legs and whispered sweet nothings about not being able to live without you. That power-hungry jerk, that selfish crawler, was petrified lest you impinge on his fucking career. The stinking bastard left you on the streets like a homeless, pregnant bitch.

How your kind, elegant soul suffered because of that injustice! You had those heavy bags crammed with encyclopaedias, from A to Mai in one hand and Maj to Z in the other – four thick, heavy volumes on each side. You lugged them through the steep streets of the city all day and arrived home exhausted and bathed in sweat, still carrying the encyclopaedias, which you had to heave up the stairs of our block of flats, five floors up, and then down again, and up, and down again. But despite all your superhuman efforts, I wouldn't let you rid yourself of me. Why didn't I let you do it? We would have been happier, both of us. You would have enjoyed your life with your lover, or lovers, because, Mum, you're the most attractive, sexiest woman I've ever met. From my earliest childhood, there was no overlooking the way men devoured you with their eyes, with all their male ganglia firing, the way they flashed seductive smiles at you, and the more daring ones, with one eyebrow raised, would venture on into the realm of allusions. But as soon as Mr Bold's glance wandered down to me, his expression changed abruptly: the enchantment swiftly ebbed away, leaving a face full of unconcealed horror. I felt so ashamed at times like that, Mum, to have embarrassed you, to have humiliated you with my presence!

I don't understand why even now, so many years after the incident in the bathroom, I still get the stupid urge to cry again. Forgive me, Mum, I know my crying is not like that of a normal human being, but I've never been normal. It's not that I haven't tried to live and to find meaning even where there is none. But it never worked. I wasn't even able to kill Kyrie, although I planned everything meticulously, just as I did with your lover. The time: midnight, when all the patients, nurses and orderlies at the sanatorium were in bed and Kyrie was returning to her room after her last round. The place: a dark corridor, and I was waiting for her behind a toilet door. The weapon: a long screwdriver I stole from the garage where we had to wash Kyrie's VW Golf as part of our 'occupational therapy'.

I forgot just one thing – that I'm so short. I needed ten centimetres more to be able to stab Kyrie with the screwdriver where I wanted to; in the heart. I also disregarded the fact that she was no walkover: Kyrie the Matron was a little surprised by my attack but in no way scared. With a quick, sure move that seemed part of a well-trained repertoire, she grabbed me by the wrist, whipped me around and pushed me to the floor. My lunge had only grazed her in the groin, and she managed to grab the broom that was leaning against the wall and brought the handle down on my face with all her might. I blacked out and all I felt was the warm blood splashing my face and filling my mouth. I only have a vague memory of what happened afterwards: the cops dragging me away and hitting me, an old doctor stitching the cuts on my face without anaesthetic and disfiguring me even more, if that's possible, and a judge sneering: 'You've got it coming to you now, midget, you're up shit creek!' If anyone had asked me if I had really been to a sanatorium and if people were really cured there, I wouldn't have known what to say. I also have a fleeting memory of a supposed lawyer pretending to be my defence counsel and arguing that I was a victim of my circumstances, which had made me a helpless multiplier of irrational violence, but I didn't care any more. I just have to admit being a bit disappointed, Mum, that you didn't come to the trial. But when they told me later that you were on holiday at the Borovets ski resort in Bulgaria – with your lover, what's more – I was glad you were able to take a break from all the mess and problems I caused you. I'd like to take this opportunity to thank your lover for the present he sent me, although it only cost eight euros (that's what it says on the box) and I did the jigsaw in just a few minutes. Twenty-piece jigsaws like that are for small kids.

But don't you worry, it's not as bad here as you might expect. They call the place a *Corrective Centre for Juveniles*, although it reminds me more of a dungeon. Still, it's not that grim. I've learnt that there are many boys here with stories like mine, lads much taller and better looking than me who are just as hapless. My cell here, unlike the 'Damned Cell', has a window with bars on it, but it is still a window. I can watch the weather through it and tell if it's sunny or cloudy, raining or snowing, and every night I can watch the stars and count them idly as I chew my potatoes; there are always boiled potatoes for dinner. If I stand on tiptoe in the cell I can even see beyond the walls of the Centre and spot people and cars going down the street. I can even see the crowns of the trees: in leaf yesterday, and with bare branches today. They say our only task here is to kill time, but I have no problem with that. I could live here in this prison for years without getting bored. The days might seem long, but viewed in sequence they actually become shorter. I'm satisfied. The food is frugal but you can rely on it – three meals a day plus a morning snack. We have compulsory PE every morning in the courtyard. You know what they say, *Mens sana in corpore sano*. Perhaps I really will succeed in strengthening my body and building up some muscles, and maybe then I will improve on the inside, too...

How long will I stay here? – until I'm nineteen. Then I'll have to leave the place, but I'll manage. I've actually heard that if I attack one of the guards I could get a few more years, and then be moved to a real prison. But don't you worry. Now that you're a safe distance away from my obnoxiousness it's only fair that you now finally enjoy love and all those other little things that make one's life fulfilled.

Just imagine, Kyrie the Matron testified at the trial – ostensibly in my defence – that I had wanted to stab her with the screwdriver because my mother hadn't given me enough warmth and affection. How despicable of her! She even mentioned my phoney father, that gutless Party functionary, as if he was the reason for you becoming unfeeling towards me. I was still in a daze from the thrashing the policemen had given me and the slapdash operation by the old doctor who first sewed my cuts without anaesthetic and only sprayed some kind of painkiller on my face afterwards; my mouth was numb and I could only mutter:

'That's not true, Matron.'

She turned around towards me – tall, slim, and a little pale without her make-up.

'Sorry, I didn't understand a word of that,' she said, and, turning back to the judge, she added: 'Poor little blighter, I really do feel sorry for him.'

I so longed to reply and slap the truth in her hypocritical mug, but I had been beaten black and blue; my ears were still ringing and my knees still shaking from the beating I'd been given, and all I was able to do in that abyss of pain was to spit. But, being so weak, I couldn't even do that properly, so the spit just oozed over my contorted blue lips. That must have made me look particularly revolting because an awkward, nauseated silence descended on the courtroom, and the policeman standing beside me grabbed me under the arm forcefully and squeamishly, the way a dog catcher nabs a mangy stray.

I'm feeling a bit jaded, Mum. So much has happened recently. And I feel better here, on the inside. There's peace and quiet, I'm hardly ever plagued by hallucinations or bad thoughts, I wake up rested, I do my PE and I have regular meals. You promise you'll come and visit me? Don't get me wrong, but there's no need for you to come all that often. Your love warms me from afar. I just need to think of you: then I can smell your delicate perfume and am rapt, just like an ugly bumblebee is intoxicated by the queen rose. Your beautiful hologram is etched deep inside me, so wherever I am and wherever you fare, you will always be with me.

This fairy tale should not be told near stagnant water

Snakelet

He found the snakelet at the very beginning of his solitary life, and now, after five years of living together, they had the same trust in each other as do close relatives. The snakelet ate out of his hand, went with him on walks through the forest – dozing in the pocket of his faded but still warm fur coat, or crawling along behind him when invigorated by the sun. On winter nights it slept long and peacefully, coiled up in a nest of twigs, leaves and moss he had made for it by the fire.

The little snake was patterned and only four inches long, at most. It enjoyed climbing along his arm, hissing joyfully with its little tongue. And it loved to lie in wait for its prey – a hypnotized bug, perhaps – and weave its hunter's dance around it.

By the end of the second year, he had taught it to recognize his whistle. Now he was trying to teach it to distinguish the short, sharp whistle which meant 'Come!' from the long, protracted one which meant 'I'm bringing you food,' and the two whistles of equal length meaning 'Lift yourself up!' – at which the snakelet would raise its head and the upper third of its body and sway from side to side.

He was happiest when it brought him his pipe. This difficult task, announced by one short and one long whistle, required the snakelet to perform several actions in sequence: to find the pipe, to pick it up with its little fangs, and to bring it to him. The snakelet would leave tiny, wet bite-marks on the stem of the pipe, and when the man lit his pipe and drew on it he felt he was imbibing a special tenderness.

Yet, after five years of seclusion, loneliness began to oppress him. While absent-mindedly stroking the curvy body of the snakelet, he realized that the blame lay in himself. He might have been offended, because people might have been nasty and unfair to him, but he had no right to be angry with them for so long. How could he forget the beautiful days of his childhood and youth? How could he forget that he had once been loved and that he himself had offended others? He was only human too, after all.

So he decided to return to the city. He put on his fur coat, slipped the snakelet into his pocket, and set off. As soon as he saw the first houses, he almost broke into a run.

But when he came face to face with the city, he sensed that invisible barrier again – the one he had felt whenever, in his solitary years, he had descended from his cave into the city in search of food. The same sense of breathlessness came over him. The city was suffocating him.

Already he was met by the astonished, derisive stares of the passers-by. His wild hair and shaggy beard, his tattered old coat, out of which his arms jutted like rusty spades, and his fearful reaction to any loud noise, made him stand out. In the eyes of the city he belonged to the class of beggars who come out at dusk to rummage through the garbage bins, glancing around nervously like hungry dogs.

By the time he made it to the first café, he was shaking like a drunk. At the last moment, before going in, he thought to take the snakelet out of his pocket. It zipped across the pavement as fast as lightning and disappeared into a crack in the wall of the nearest house. There, in the stone crevice, it calmed down. Its friend's disquiet had unsettled the little creature. Instinctively, it felt safe in the dark. It waited.

In the café, the bar keeper and five or six guests – all men – were listening to a football match on the radio. The shrill, eunuch-like voice of the commentator, combined with the shouting and cursing of the sweaty men made him seek the furthest table. He sat huddled there on the chair, covering his ears with his broad hands, until the feel of his own skin gradually calmed him down.

Only then did he notice the fellow at the next table. He was sitting away from the men with the radio and gazing peacefully out into the street. A pair of crutches rested against the chair beside him. Turning from the window, the fellow smiled and said, 'Nice day today.'

He went on talking in a lively, rambling way about the coming of spring, pollution in the cities, and the impossibility of true communication. It turned out that both men harboured the same bitterness and the same contempt for crowds.

At first, our man just nodded in agreement, later tossing in the occasional 'yes', 'that's right', and 'I think so too'. But when the fellow moved on to the problem of friendship, he felt he needed to interrupt his monologue, 'where can you find sincerity? People are selfish and care only for their own interests.'

Unconsciously, the two men moved closer to each another. He was now resting his arms on the next table, while the like-minded fellow was leaning toward him. All of a sudden, our man exclaimed: 'I've got something to show you – a true friend!'

And as the fellow sent him an almost cheerful look of approval, our man gave a short, sharp whistle. The football fans by the radio turned and cast him angry glances.

The snakelet did not respond. The man had never asked it to enter a room full of people before; he had taught it to be wary of them. It decided to stay in its hole.

'Please hear me and come out!' he begged. 'Just this once!' He whistled again, now with an air of desperation. His whistle brought a tirade of curses from the other men, and the bar keeper yelled: 'Shut up, you dunce! Can't you see we're listening to the game?'

The fellow from the next table scratched himself behind his ear. 'Sorry, but I don't understand,' he said.

Just then, the head of the snakelet appeared under the front door. Warmth filled his heart. 'There he is!' he whispered, 'He's coming.'

But the very next instant, as if in slow motion, the curiosity on his neighbour's face changed to revulsion and his hand grasped murderously for the crutch.

The Man with One Wing

Once there was a man who had one wing. Unlike an angel's wings, which grow out of its back, this man's wing was in the place of his right arm, and unlike a bird's it had a flexible elbow, which he rested on as he sat on a large rock and stared away into the distance as if looking out to sea: but there was no sea, only a hillside clearing with a few scattered trees.

For the man with one wing, that summer was one of the most depressing of his life. He was haunted by a sense of emptiness and futility, a feeling heightened on those July afternoons by the stale, sour smell rising from the hot city, that sticky mass of cars and people constantly creeping like a foul treacle and defiling even the narrowest alleyways. The man with one wing sat on that rock halfway up Mount Vodno and looked into the sky, following a cloud that was forever changing shape, like every restless puff of vapour, and he thought: *Just look at that cloud. It can do whatever it wants, while I...*

At that very moment, a bird came flying up. It was an eagle, as large as in fairy tales, and it obscured the sun and the restless cloud. The huge bird descended to within a yard of the man with one wing, hovering in the air, and looked straight at him.

'What do you want of me?' asked the man with one wing in the shadow of the eagle.

It replied with a question: 'Why are you still on the ground?'

'Can't you see I only have one wing? What can I do if I'm crippled like this? Without a right hand, I can't even wank. But why have you come? Did I call you?'

'I've come to tell you something very important. You may not want to hear it, but that can't be helped: I am your cousin.'

'What?!'

'All right, not a first cousin. Perhaps four or five times removed. But we are related. Our common relation, the Grey Eagle – that is your father, and a distant uncle of mine – once accidentally brushed your mother with his wing and she fell pregnant.'

'Even if that's true, what does it have to do with me now?'

'You are the one in whom bird and man are united. Moreover, you are the only son of the Grey Eagle, and he is the king of the eagles. He is dying and asks me to bring you to him. He wants to see you.'

And so the man with one wing climbed onto the eagle's back and the huge bird bore him away. As fast as the wind it flew, swiftly passing mountains, lakes and rivers, and soon they reached a lofty mountain peak covered in snow. Here there was a large eyrie, with a throne in the middle and a white fireplace, whose flames burned with a strange light, white and pure. Despite the snow and ice all around, it was pleasantly warm inside the eyrie. This was the home of the Grey Eagle.

The great bird sat, or rather lay slumped, atop the throne. Not even the fire could allay the fever that raged in his once mighty, kingly frame.

'My son,' he spoke to the man with one wing, 'tonight I leave for the land of our ancestors. I do not wish to go, but I have no choice – my time has come. I have never troubled you before, but since my last hour is drawing near I have resolved to share the secret that I am your father.'

'I know that already. It seems rather obvious, doesn't it?'

'But there's something more. With my death, the throne of the eagles will become vacant. It awaits you, and it is for you to choose if you will ascend it. May the birds in your right half and the men in your left decide your course.'

'I don't know what to say. You've really caught me unprepared.'

'You must decide. I am growing weaker, ever weaker, and I must know your answer. Will you stay here or go back to live among men? And one other thing: how is your mother?'

'She is well, for her age.'

'How old is she exactly?'

'Seventy-five.'

'That old already? It seems like just yesterday that I brushed her with my wing. You should have seen me in my prime.'

The man with one wing failed to notice that his father had tried to soften the situation with humour. He still didn't understand what was going on and stood there gawping, his mind a muddle. The Grey Eagle lifted his heavy head with visible effort and spoke to him for the last time:

'Tell me, my son, will you be my heir? Will you become the king of all birds? I'm glad I sent for you, my son...'

'I... I...,' the man with one wing stuttered, but the Grey Eagle could no longer hear him. He had passed out into the narrow way separating the two worlds, where the sounds of this world become ever fainter and are soon gone.

And so, without really wanting to, the man with one wing became king of the eagles, to the acclaim of the entire aquiline assembly.

'How can I possibly rule when I can't even fly, let alone soar up to the heights?' the man wondered, sitting on the throne of stone that now struck him as being very similar to the rock halfway up Mount Vodno, which he had climbed to escape the city before this remarkable episode with his father, the Grey Eagle. But since he was now king, which meant that all the eagles were now at his service, he ordered for a large, light and powerful wing to be made for him as soon as possible and that it be affixed, gently but firmly, to the left side of his back. He noticed that giving the order came easily to him, and no sooner had he spoken than his wish was fulfilled!

He was no longer a man with one wing but a king with two wings. Or rather, two wings and one arm. His left arm, now solitary, white and oddly beautiful in its helplessness, could be used for noble deeds such as bearing the sceptre or leafing through a travel book illustrated with etchings. The places on the man's back where his wings were, the natural one and the new artificial one, pulsated and tingled most pleasantly.

'Now I can take to the sky!' he cried and launched into flight.

Yes, it was as if all the energy had returned to his body, and as he breathed in the air of the heights – so intoxicating, so liberating – he felt he was bending the skies to his will and seizing life in a completely different way to before. The waters of the mountain rivers rushed, babbling through forested dells far below him; houses, even large buildings looked like little models from a children's game. He, the eagle king, felt proud and majestic, and he laughed loud and long above the clouds: 'Ha, ha, ha! Ha, ha, ha!'

He flew to see his mother, who was not astonished to see him as an eagle. In fact, she seemed to be relieved.

'You don't have to explain anything. I understand,' she heartened him.

His mother, who was not seventy-five but actually eighty, could finally be proud of her son. He wore his wings like a royal cloak draped over his left arm.

'Mother, so far I have caused you nothing but trouble with my restlessness and complexes, but now I am strong and self-confident. Tell me, is there a wish I can fulfil to gratify you for once?'

His mother was quiet and thought for a minute or more, and then she spoke in a rush, like a river suddenly released: 'My son, it's true you were awkward and idle for many years and caused me much pain and embarrassment. My friends gossiped about you time and again, and afterwards I couldn't sleep for nights on end. I'm not saying it was your fault – perhaps we had to go through it all because fate decided it should be that way. But we cannot change the past. And when I see you now, so tall and handsome, I could cry... with happiness...'

'Don't cry, mother!'

'I have become old and sentimental, but it will pass. Let me think of a wish you could fulfil for me.'

'Tell me, mother, tell me!'

'Ah, I know. Last night, or the night before, I dreamed of a girl. She was beautiful and she lived by the shore of a mountain lake, so high that in winter the moss was covered in six inches of snow.'

'It suits me that it should be high up. Since I've had two wings I've become very fond of heights.'

'Yes, I believe you. But there was something else in the dream, too, some little problem. Just let me just try and remember what it was.'

'Don't strain, mother. Whatever it is, I shall overcome the problem.'

Later, back on his throne, the former man with one wing and current king of the eagles steeled his resolve: *A man, even one with two wings, must follow the path fate has chosen for him without turning aside. He must walk it to its end and then, if he can, he must understand his role in the wheel of life.*

He ordered all his winged subjects to begin searching near and far for a girl of indisputable beauty living by the shore of a high mountain lake. All the eagles immediately set off to the four corners of the world, and our hero, not wishing to sit alone and bored in his eyrie, joined in the search himself.

He flew long and hard until, after a whole week, one day at high noon he saw a dark-blue lake at the peak of a tall mountain. Three swans were bathing in its clean, clear waters, and three dresses lay on the shore. *Why are there swans this high up? And what are these dresses doing here?* He was right to wonder. He hid behind a snow-covered pine tree and peered out: one of the swans emerged from the water, shook its feathers and began to change into a beautiful girl. Shivering with cold, she donned her golden dress and ran barefoot across the snow, down to a stone cottage. The second swan came out and the same process was repeated. It too turned into a beautiful girl who, predictably, put on her silver dress and ran after her sister.

But before the third swan could leave the lake, the eagle king sneaked out from behind the pine tree and snatched the white dress. Terrified, the swan paddled back over the water and spoke to him in the gentle voice of a girl: 'Please give me my dress back.'

'All right, come up onto the shore and take it. I'll hang it on this pine branch and go round behind the tree.'

The swan-girl thought to herself: *I'll grab my dress and start running.*

But the eagle king thought: As soon as she comes nearer she's mine!

The swan-girl ran up onto the shore, making for the branch where her white dress was hanging. She moved fast, but the eagle king was faster. He leapt in front of her and seized her in his eagle's embrace. At that instant, her body began to change and shed its feathers, first revealing her long, white, fragrant neck, and soon a shock of blonde curls danced in front of him and tickled his nose. He was no longer touching the body of a swan but that of a young woman, whose skin breathed and shone much more suggestively than the feathers. He took half a step backwards, less in shyness than from the desire to feast his eyes on her. As her body was gradually exposed to him, disclosing its beauty inch by inch, his excitement grew and redoubled; he relished the sight but was aware that there were enticing secret chambers and shady gardens yet to be discovered. He was still holding her in a half-embrace. Was it just his imagination that her velvety eyes, darker than her hair, grew large and moist when his old right wing brushed against the hard nipple of her now fully human, orange-shaped breast? As he hugged her nymphean body, his wing feathers reacted with unseen sensitivity and puffed up like the plumage of a strutting rooster.

He so revelled in the view that he scarcely heard her softly spoken words: 'Would you mind passing me my dress?'

Only then did he realize that she was wet and shivering with cold. He handed her the dress, and as she raised her arms to pull it over her head she revealed all her feminine beauty: her slender waist, wide white hips and bushy mound. It took him a few moments to come to his senses and understand what she was saying, because as soon as she had put on her dress she began telling her story. It seemed strangely familiar (had he heard it from his mother or someone even older?).

Eliza, for that was the name of this gentle yet voluptuous creature, and her sisters, all of them of noble birth, had become entangled in the dark magic of their stepmother. She was in fact a witch, who had enchanted their frivolous father, and then one afternoon when he was away she cast a bewitched shirt over each of the girls and turned them into swans. So no one would see their misery, they flew far away to a lake at the peak of a mountain. And so they had been living here as swans for seven years. They could only return to human form at noon, and never for more than one hour, after which they turned back into swans.

'And I so yearned for a second wing,' our hero let slip, but Eliza was carried away in relating her own sad story and didn't quite catch his comment.

'Yes, I also yearn to be what I was... there is a way we can be saved, but it would be such a long, hard road for our redeemer,' she sighed.

'Tell me how! Tell me right away!'

'I don't know if it's proper...'

'Proper or not, I want only to make you happy, you and myself.'

'All right: you must not smile or speak a word to anyone for a whole year.'

'That will be far from easy, to be sure, but if needs be I will neither smile nor speak a single word. My eagles might not understand at first, but I'll find a way. There's mime, after all.'

'You're making a big sacrifice for me. But that's not all. There's another very difficult task.'

'I will face the challenge, I can't give up now. But why are you being so self-conscious? There's no need, although it makes me even fonder of you.'

'Then I'll tell you: in the year ahead, as well as not speaking or smiling, you must knit three shirts. For me and my sisters.'

'Three shirts? Now that really amazes me. I've never done any women's work in my life. Men don't knit, you know.'

'There's something more I have to tell you. The shirts must be made of stinging nettles. Now you see all the trials and tribulations you have to undergo to save me from the spell. Me and my sisters.'

'Eliza, your solidarity is moving. I must admit I don't understand these sacrifices, maybe because I've been such a loner till now.'

'It's a tradition of my people. According to our legends, the world was knitted into creation. Divine knitting needles patiently created all these mountains with their holy tarns and lakes and snow-capped peaks, all these dark-green forests, as well as all the cabbages, blueberries and potatoes, the cows, wolves and eagles.'

'Eagles?'

'Yes, all the beasts and birds are made of divine yarn.'

'And people too?'

'All of us are connected by the threads of the divine knitting-women. The whole universe is made of those strong, invisible threads whose task is to preserve its equilibrium: the balance between the external and the internal, between the skies and the deep, between male and female. The women of our people therefore keep our clothes white by washing them in the clean, cold mountain lakes and streams. But –,' Eliza sighed, 'there are also witches, like my stepmother, who attack and unpick the fabric of the universe. That's why she tangled the threads of the divine yarn and turned us into swans.'

'Then it looks as if some wicked witch has been at work on me, too.'

Eliza's cheeks, already aglow from the excitement of storytelling, now turned crimson: 'But your appearance... how can I put it...the way you look really suits you. It makes you strong and manly. Oh, my dear, will you be able to make this sacrifice for my sake? For our future happiness and all the pleasures that await us? From the moment you say "yes" you'll have to hold your silence for a whole year, you won't be allowed to smile, and you'll have to knit those nettle shirts.' She straightened her grapefruit-shaped breasts, which seemed to burgeon even more under her wet dress. 'I so much want to believe you'll succeed. After all... sorry for having to mention it... but you do only have one arm.'

At that, his weak left arm clasped her to him: 'At the risk of sounding blunt, Liza, why can't we... while we're mulling over all this... why can't you and I get to know each other a bit better now, you know.

'There will be time for everything, my love. If our plan works, there will be joys you have never dreamed of. But now you must say "yes" and refrain from words and smiles for a whole year – a year of knitting, knitting and more knitting until you see us flying back to you and the finished shirts.'

A 'yes' slipped from his mouth, and then there was no going back.

And so the eagle king, with a heavy heart, parted with Eliza and flew to see his mother in silence. She noticed straight away that something was wrong.

'You've gone very quiet, my son. Much has happened to you of late. Here, show me what troubles you – draw it in the air with your wings, or with your hand, or with your eyes. I'm your mother, I'll understand.'

So he started to wave, wheel around, hop up and down, and open his eyes wide and squeeze them shut again. It would have seemed most peculiar to anyone else, but not to his mother, who gradually, by a logic known only to her, began to understand what he was trying to say.

'It won't be easy at all. I remember being told something like that in a dream, but you were impatient and didn't listen to me. Still, I'll do all I can to help. It will be hard going until you learn to knit properly, especially at the beginning, but as soon as you've knitted your first stitches it will become easier and you'll be surprised how quickly it goes. For you, my son, things are a bit more complicated with just your one arm, and even your father, for all his experience, was not particularly good at using his wings. But let's not complain. Sit down now and listen. In one of your hands – the left one in your case – you take an old-fashioned knitting needle with a hook at the end. Nod to me if you understand. Good. And then you'll use your right wing like this to hold the thread and wrap it around. Yes, just like that. First make one loop, slowly, and now pull the thread with the hand holding the needle and make a braid, a plait. I know it's hard, my son, but if you can make that braid you know all there is to know. Come on, one more time. Don't get frustrated. In time, you'll find it so easy you'll be able to do it with a nail. You pick up the thread and pass it through. Pick up and pass through. Take a little break now, and I'll teach you the two kinds of stitches, the knit stitch and the purl stitch. Nod to me if you understand.'

And so began the eagle king's long year of knitting, and the toil was made even more onerous by using nettles for yarn and having to abstain from speaking and smiling. But, as he expected, it was his subjects who posed the biggest problem. And they had reason enough to be resentful. Him not smiling worried them the least; eagles, as we know, are not famous for their sense of humour. But him not speaking made for a serious problem. If only his reason had been pride and loftiness they would have forgiven him – he was the king of the eagles, after all. But hour after hour, day after day and month after month he just sat on his throne of stone, flightless, wordless, and knitted! He flew only after midnight, and then it was to cemeteries to pick nettles for knitting those shirts. The fingers on his left hand were covered with blisters, but he kept on knitting in silence with a dull look in his eyes. The eagles saw this as complete and utter decadence.

They began to whisper about him, and soon they were gossiping openly. Still he held his tongue and knitted. Now the eagles called an urgent assembly. Angry voices went up: 'We are sick of this ruler! Oust him!' He was calmly knitting the third shirt, with the other two lying finished beside him. 'This is an insult!' 'He's mocking us!' 'What a disgrace!' 'Depose him!' 'Lynch him!' The threats became more severe by the minute as a circle of eagles drew tighter around him.

All of a sudden, the sky darkened and three white swans came down to land in the small space that remained around him and meekly bowed their long necks. He quickly cast the shirts over their heads and, to the wonder of all those present, except himself, the swans turned into Eliza and her two sisters. What a beautiful sight! The girls were gorgeous, and their shirts were like tunics that showed off their svelte yet curvaceous bodies. Tears of joy rolled down Eliza's cheeks as she told the curious listeners of the sisters' rousing odyssey, caused by their stepmother-witch and her bad magic, and the ordeal the eagle king had gone through for her sake.

'Move back, all of you. Give her room to breathe!' the eagles now heard their ruler's voice for the first time in a year, and it was as resolute and confident as before. They made way for him, and he went up to Eliza and hugged her tight. He began to caress her and soon noticed that, instead of a left arm, she still had a wing: 'your poor arm! I've failed you. I didn't finish the last sleeve.'

'Don't be sad. I'll wear this swan's wing with pride, as a symbol of your selfless love. And we'll complement each other when we do what lovers do.'

They finished the court and family formalities with the king's ministers as quickly as they could. Then his mother (who reminded all who couldn't escape her company of her vital role in the knitting saga) and the sisters all undressed and went to bed.

'What's so funny?' he asked, a little snubbed, when he saw Eliza grinning.

'The birthmark, my dear – the birthmark on your penis. Now, just before we get intimate, I was checking that it's on the right-hand side.'

'What the...'

'You see, there's a belief among our people that those with a birthmark on the left lean one way, so to speak, and those with it on the right lean another... so I just wanted to check. But now we can make love. My kisses will put a smile back on your face.'

Her voice went husky, as if there was a fluttering bird in her throat that wanted to escape. 'Oh my God,' the man with one wing muttered before getting down to business. And it was much better than in his wildest dreams.

And so the two of them lived happily for many, many years, until the end of their lives. Especially him. Eliza watched over him until her death. He was eighty when she died, having inherited his mother's longevity, and his son, the heir to the throne, made sure he lacked nothing. Even his fading memory became a boon, for he felt carefree, as if he lived in a second childhood filled with fantasies and mythical creatures from distant, fairy-tale worlds. In old age, when he became ever more simple-minded, his imagination gained two powerful wings for antics and frivolity.

Now and again, accompanied by some of his caring servants, he would climb a hill that seemed strangely familiar (where did he know it from?) and sit on a rock there amidst a somehow familiar clearing. Taking the occasional bite of his favourite Turkish delight with coconut, tasty and soft enough for his toothless jaws, he would stare at the sky, where large and small clouds were in flight, changing shape from a horse into an elephant, an elephant into a train, a train into a snake – and so on, and so forth, almost without end.

The Dance of the Coloured Handkerchiefs

One day, a colourful silk handkerchief got angry with its mother, ran away from home and set off into the wide world in search of a boy or girl with a runny nose. It was very small and didn't yet know how to wipe someone's nose; it didn't even know what a child looked like; but still, it left on the long journey.

It wandered for a long time until it came to a pretty yellow house with a red chimney and swirls of smoke coming out. The brave little handkerchief thought the house was a boy or girl, and the chimney its nose.

'No, no. I am a house,' it corrected the little traveller. 'But come inside and perhaps you will find a child.'

Without further ado, the handkerchief went in and found itself in a large, well-lit room with a big round lamp in the corner.

'That must be the head of the child, but where is its nose?' our little hero asked itself when it saw the smooth, attractive lamp.

'No, no. I am a lamp. But just wait a minute and André will come home from school.'

And, sure enough, a few moments later a tousled little head ran into the room. It had restless locks, a cheerful smile with a row of tiny white stones, and a snotty nose like a little potato that's been in the pan for too long.

'I've found you, I've found you,' the handkerchief piped. 'Let me wipe your nose!'

André blew his nose into it, laughed a hearty little laugh, and snatched the handkerchief. 'You're just what I need, but for something quite different. You can help me in my new act.'

Later, in the long evening by the fire, André told his new friend that he was the son of the great magician Petronius and that tomorrow they would start practicing a new act together – *The Dance of the Coloured Handkerchiefs.*

So the wayward handkerchief became a great star in the circus tent and beyond. Every evening, for an enthusiastic audience, it vanished into a magic hat and then flew out again as a white dove. Such a life was exciting for the handkerchief, and it enjoyed being pampered: it was washed, ironed, and even doused with exotic perfumes. At night it slept close to André's heart, in the upper left-hand pocket of his juggler's costume. In the meantime it made it up with its mother, and she became very, very proud of it. She all but forgot her anger at it having run away from home.

Still, even in the moments of glamour and shine, when the circus tent was filled with cheers and applause, the colourful silk handkerchief would look up yearningly at André's nose:

Oh, if only I could wipe it one more time!

Human, all too Human

4.
Once out of nature I shall never take
My bodily form from any natural thing,
But such a form as Grecian goldsmiths make
Of hammered gold and gold enamelling
To keep a drowsy Emperor awake;
Or set upon a golden bough to sing
To lords and ladies of Byzantium
Of what is past, or passing, or to come.

WILLIAM BUTLER YEATS, *Sailing to Byzantium*

On the opposite bank, from the depths of the forests steaming after the rain, a flock of birds shot up almost vertically into the sky. Their cries echoed through the mists and died away to the nervous looks of the men and horses on this side of the river, half sinking in the whitish sighs of the mushy soil – they felt like nameless members of a wild horde of centaurs wandering aimlessly before the wrath of the Lord of the Netherworld.

They had been following the river for two whole days and nights. At first they fooled themselves into thinking that the babbling water would lead them somewhere. Now, the eerie reverberating shrieks of the unreal shadows flitting overhead made the waters seem immobile and ominous, like a dark-green bog.

'These pathless wilds are no place for a Byzantine noble!' the rider muttered as he gazed into the enchanted emptiness and struggled to calm his nervous animal. In the cramped muscles and cold sweat of his stallion he felt his own madness looming, the intertwining of earthly and devilish roads, when the reins were to be handed over to the *Other*, the mad one, who is detached from reason. In the year of great darkness, the rider recognized the signs – symbols from no book and beyond the order of letters:

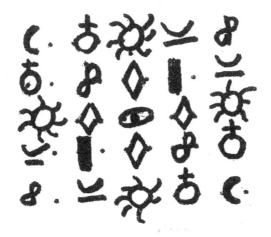

'Here lies the hidden breath of our ancestors,' the Syrian said as his bony forefinger traced over the symbols. 'They carved their secret into the philosophers' stone and then disappeared. Thunder and lightning signalled that it was time to leave. Who were they? For the deities, sunny days are migratory birds. A mere blink and it is autumn already. Silence. But the stone protects their wounds from the oblivion of posterity. Reach out your hand. Can you feel the passion it emanates? Do you think the stone is a bloodless thing that cannot suffer? Do you desire it?' the Easterner asked, holding the rider's hand between his own and the amulet and raising his eyes beneath his dangling locks of white hair. 'You are a nobleman. Your retinue is of proud and warlike men. But I am not afraid of the sword. I left my fear in Beirut, in the ashes of what was once my home. And it was foretold that I am the only one who can hand down the stone with a blessing. I, the descendant of Seth who presaged the hour of Robert Guiscard's death. It was said that the stone would pass through hundreds of lives. My life and yours are but little eddies of water in its inexhaustible flow.'

And with that the Syrian grinned, making the youngest, beard-less henchman give a dry, nervous cough; he was still terrified by stories about the bloodthirsty *gello* in the wastes that sucked the blood of children and left them hanging empty, in the way a spider does with its prey. His cough electrified the heavy air and broke the stifling silence:

'Do not deceive yourself into believing it will protect you. At least not in the way fools who adorn themselves with gold chains imagine it will. This world where we sell our princesses to the bar-barians for a peace that won't last for more than two years is a fragile one. No one can pretend to innocence. The hordes from the East are like a hydra with a hundred heads, and the warri-ors from the North are an icy wind from the endless steppes that ravages the Holy City. Until now, the Empire has been able to play off its ferocious opponents one against another, but for how much longer? The stone will not help you if only your eyes give you satisfaction, if you see nothing other than the dark surface of light. But if the light looks for a refuge inside you, perhaps it will impart to you some of its wisdom. Its portents sometimes stand forth unpredictably like green moss on bare, beaten rock. Let us recall: although he had been warned that the first to set foot on Trojan soil would instantly be killed, the son of Laertes was the first to leap from the ship – he threw his shield ashore before jumping himself. He remained alive and won fame.'

The rider imagined the intermingling blood of the heroes that flowed from the eyeholes in their bronze helmets and turned the river red, while a new seed sprouted in their slashed eyes; battle-cries and screams of agony merged and were borne away with the waves – the proud rage of warriors who overcame their hubris; grey-bearded veteran and fiery youngster alike, now slain, were joined in the eternal embrace of Charon's waters. All of us gathered here have a Patroclus immersed in ultimate loneliness, silently yearning for the sun, beneath which we would toil day and night just so as to feel the touch of its rays once more. The morning after the battle saw a pack of wolves feeding on the bodies of the dead, which were dusted with snow: a truly primeval scene. The rider had the same feeling as when the northern barbarians danced their silent dance with the girls – the young warrior tempting the girl to follow him, putting her through lively steps, ever faster and faster, each spin more demanding than the last. That was a celebration of hip-thrusting vitality, while here death reigned, but in both scenes the light that flooded over the figures and the landscape (like the bright shafts that pierce the gauze screens and fill the womb of the bedroom) was like heavenly grace that altered the seemingly ordered relationship on earth between a figure and its voice, between the object and its movement – the blissful caress of our ethereal Father. Yes, the rider could feel the infinite kindness and immeasurable power that extended both above and below the clouds; he could feel the dancing curls of the enslaved girls, the flash of creation everywhere.

The derisive, raspy voice of the Syrian brought the rider back to the stark reality of the cold vapours on the river-bank, cutting the serene surface of his idealized vision almost painfully.

'The one who had the stone before me mixed wisdom with madness. He was known by the name of Constantine Anastasis, a learned patrician sent from the capital to administer our province. They say the hot sun stirred the dreams of Eastern rulers – vain fantasies of grandeur and power in the new Empire, dreams sustained by gigantic statues of themselves. There he asks for more and takes more, as he reclines on his wide swing, surrounded by exotic plants. So it was that Constantine too, having learnt of the stone, began to be tormented by mad visions of all the things he could do if he possessed it, although he tried to resist its pull. He returned to his books and recited long prayers, but among the pages of writing and between the icons he would always see the stone. He began searching for it, surreptitiously at first, then ever more anxiously; and at the thirtieth sunset, before the tombs in the apse of the martyrium, one of his spies whispered to him that the stone was hidden in the house of the merchant Moshe ben Azzai, in the Jewish quarter. So Constantine ordered that the merchant be brought before him, although, in the spirit of the Emperor's magnanimous law permitting Jews to work even in the court administration, he decided to welcome him with a smile.'

The rider pictured the tense body of the administrator poorly concealed in his emerald-green, velvet tunic, with a forced grin on his face; he also imagined the stooping figure of the Jew, who, fearing the worst, had bad farewell to the jokes at the family table and the solemn murmur of the synagogue prayers as he was led from his leather-goods store to the palace. By the time he arrived before the potentate he was almost cleansed of his fear, and he was only hunched because of his inherited arthritis, not due to servility in the face of this despised tormentor. Yes, the rider thought of how the merchant must have mocked his haughty Christian masters who were too busy with their clothes, coiffures and scheming between races at the Hippodrome to think of the common weal.

Once again, the hoarse voice of the Syrian cut through the living skein of the rider's imaginings.

'The Jew never used the stone. They say his rabbi advised him against it, citing the words of Rabbi Hillel: "Do not strive to stand out in the community!" and "Do not believe in yourself until the day of your death!" He stressed the example of Simon ben Zoma, known simply as Ben Zoma and famed for his perception and kindness, revered even in the proverb, "Whoever dreams of Ben Zoma is assured of wisdom", although he later got carried away with his arcane studies, becoming engrossed in Pardes, and took leave of his senses. Despite this advice, Moshe ben Azzai was unable to part with the wondrous stone and kept it in a casket in a secret compartment in the wall known only to he and his wife. Every evening he would lock himself in his room, open the casket and stare at the stone, enchanted. Even when Constantine inflicted the severest torture, Moshe refused to reveal the location of the stone. So Constantine, no stranger to perfidious cunning, ordered his guards to bring Moshe's wife and children to the underground torture-chamber. Instead of their father, they found a disfigured body, with chains cutting into the mangled, raw flesh; it writhed and whined from what must have once been a face, with one eye gouged out and the other frenzied with unbearable pain. Moshe's obedient wife Rachel, despite having been brought up on histories of her ancestors' sufferings, could not long stand the mad despair in her beloved husband's eye, which no longer recognized her. Constantine Anastasis thus became the owner of the stone.

'He hung it around his neck. When he appeared before his servants the next morning, they say his hair had gone grey and his eyes were wild. They saw him riding through the fields, his purple cloak fluttering behind him. And, spurring his horse into a furious gallop, he disappeared before the eyes of the dismayed soldiers standing along the city walls.'

The rider saw the tense face of his youngest henchman again and thought how ebullient young men were misjudged: even if given to wanton dissipation and pleasure seeking in the cities, they were actually torn by restlessness and an abortive search for meaning.

'Constantine never returned,' the Syrian continued. 'First they found his horse roaming wild, and later, in a forest clearing, they came across his lifeless body. His skull was broken. Rumour spread that the horse's name was Theophilus, like he who sold his soul to the devil and signed the contract with his own blood.'

'And what of the stone?' The hiss of his own voice sounded to him like a muffled echo from hell. 'How did you come by it?'

The Syrian stared at the rider with goggling, bloodshot eyes: 'They say the horse was possessed by the soul of the tortured Jew. A dumb animal could not have aimed so accurate a hoof blow right in the middle of its owner's forehead. Surely it was guided by a human hand.'

The Syrian's voice seemed to quaver – he was an old man – or perhaps it faltered to a whisper because of the threatening moment itself, which stunned all those present like a clenched fist:

'When I grabbed the stone and felt its pores against mine, I was a young man in an unstoppable rush: as tall as you are, strong and thirsting for life. And now...'

His withered, decrepit hand held out the stone. The noble message carved into it, the message from the people of the golden race – those gods in human form who had lived and loved in a world of white unicorns – was destined to be handed down through the greed and impetuousness of their sordid descendants: Moshe ben

Azzai, the patrician Constantine, the poor Syrian, the rider himself, and his young henchman enchantedly devouring the stone with covetous eyes – all of them prisoners of their own baseness.

The rider's father, once an admirer of Plato, had whispered to him madly from his deathbed, scratching his hair as if he had lice:

'Look at those figs your mother brought in. They look lovely and juicy, you probably think. But inside? They're a rich royal purple, but they stink. And how! She's poisoning me, son. See that thing floating in my soup? Your mother – that bitch said it was fresh fish: nice, wholesome chunks with roe, enough to make your mouth water. But when I cut into the fish and smelt it, it stank.'

His father was convinced that his most devoted soulmate – she who had suffered with him through the hard years of exile on barren islands, who had encouraged and counselled him, who had borne him two sons and raised them with pride and warmth – was poisoning him. Yes, his own father, that paragon of learning and wisdom, had been unable to escape the mark of the beast. What hope was there then for him, so much commoner than his father? Self-imposed exile, perhaps? But where? His father had had a home, a library and leisurely, warm evenings to read and explain animal fables to him, and still he had succumbed. But what did he have? His parents' dilapidated house with no one to look after it! Ever since those who called themselves guardians of the faith, with necklaces of wild boar's teeth hanging from their fat necks, had sacked the Imperial City and sullied its squares, hurling curses and gnawed bones in their endless feasts, he was not sure they would stop at breaking down the gates and pillaging the next time. He had his rank of *Pronoiar*, but what was it worth to be a minor military commander in troubled times such as these? So far he had managed to evade all the accusations and conspiracies, but he knew he would be sucked into them in the end.

Perhaps God had made him childless so he could more easily isolate himself from everything, except from the fragile defence of thought. If it was his lot in life for loss to outweigh joy, did his appropriation of the divine dancer's passioned imprint in the soft stone not portend his final demise? What if he were to cast it into the deepest cave or bury it in the furthest desert? Oh, how power-less commands were in this life! He had pursued the Syrian across the entire Empire, scarcely halting to rest, and now, having finally caught up with him, he took the carved stone calmly, almost grudg-ingly. Should he give it straight to his young henchman, whose sharp look was piercing his back like a blade? Or smile victori-ously and conceal it in his bosom? It didn't matter. The opaque eye at the centre of the stone watched him coldly – he was an ant, an insignificant speck in the impersonality of time. The next day, or in ten years time, he would be replaced by some other little particle: one naïve or crafty or wretched, but equally meaningless – human, all too human.

This fairy tale is to be told to an animated-film fan

The Round Trip of a Shadow

Based on the story of the same name by Dimitar Solev
(1930-2003)

Scene 1:

Krum, a man with the appearance of a sixty-year-old but is actually several years younger, walks along one of Skopje's streets before the big earthquake of 1963. He is wearing an old railwayman's coat and carrying a hessian sack of soil as big as a saddle on his shoulders. A tender sapling with a few delicate leaves peeps from the mouth of the sack, like from a flowerpot. Now the shadow of a child appears beside Krum and scampers around; it dashes away from him, looks at passers-by and watches the double-decker bus heading down the street. As Krum walks on and the child-shadow runs past him, soon to come back again, one or two small leaves grow on the branch of the sapling.

Finally Krum arrives at the cemetery, along a path with deep furrows in the black earth. Mount Vodno can be clearly seen above the cemetery, overlooking the city. The shadow of the child peers curiously at the Christian and Jewish graves, stops for a moment, and then continues running around. Bird chatter. Krum arrives at a grave, some of whose letters can be recognized, but not the numbers. He takes the sapling, a flask of water and a trowel out of the sack. He digs a hole, plants the sapling and waters it from the flask. The shadow of the child helps him with the planting, although Krum is not aware of it.

An old woman in black, squats beside one of the graves nearby. Her lament is heard. Krum does not react, but the child-shadow turns towards her and listens.

47

Krum, older than in the last scene, but in the same worn-out coat plods along one of Skopje's streets (perhaps the same one as before) soon after the earthquake. The houses are full of cracks, the badly damaged ones are being demolished, while others are simply missing and large new buildings are going up in their place. Krum is carrying the same old sack, which looks bigger than before; perhaps because of the young tree, which has grown and now has branches, leaves and a few blossoms. The child-shadow is here, the same age as before, climbing and playing in the branches of the tree, although Krum doesn't feel its weight. But his step is different now – slower and stiffer, mechanical.

He arrives at the cemetery, and it seems different to the last one. There are more graves, some of them fresh and in neat, regular rows. The contours of a tall factory can be seen in the background, and white dust from the new cement works falls on the cemetery. Aeroplanes roar as they take off at the nearby airport, and one flies directly overhead.

Krum comes up to a grave in the middle of one of the rows, sighs in anguish and sits down on the slab. The name 'Mitrush' can clearly be seen, but the years are still hazy. The child-shadow sits down next to Krum, leans its head on his knees and watches him with interest. From up close, the wrinkles on the old man's face are furrowed like the bark of a tree. Krum gets up with effort and starts to take the tree out of the sack. He strains and struggles, since the tree is no longer so small. The child-shadow tries to help him. In the end, with visible pain, Krum manages to tear the tree out of the sack, as if he was ripping it out of his very own self. With great effort, breathing heavily, he plants it and waters it with drops from the flask.

A lament is heard from far away. The silhouette of an old woman in a black headscarf can be seen between the rows of graves. The child-shadow takes Krum by the hand, but he doesn't notice and looks towards the old woman instead.

SCENE 3:

Krum, now very old and already bent with the weight of years, trudges along one of Skopje's streets. Its appearance has changed completely – new building after new building, advertising boards crammed into every empty spot, gaudy shop windows and noise from the dense, never-ending traffic. Krum moves with difficulty, hardly seeming to lift his legs as he walks, as if he is stuck to the pavement and has to push himself along. The child-shadow, still of the same age, is running and dashing about even more than before: it gazes into shop windows, goes in and out of stores, climbs onto the back of the sculpture of a bull and rides it.

Slowly, very slowly, Krum draws close to what seems like a third cemetery. Now we see that his body is not only stooped, but also deformed. The noise of the cars barely subsides as he drags himself along the roads of the cemetery, which is now a veritable necropolis with broad avenues, streets and narrow lanes; the child-shadow runs and kicks pebbles along them, and the panorama of the overcrowded, smog-choked city of the living throbs in the background.

Now we see that Krum's body is turning into a tree. There is no sack any more and the tree is simply growing out of his body, with its branches sticking through his worn-out coat as if through the cracks of an old pot. Krum and the child-shadow arrive at the grave.

There is a gravestone in the form of a cross and now the letters can be seen – 'Our dear Mitrush', as well as the years 1951-1960.

The child nudges Krum to step up to the grave and stand there. The final transformation begins – Krum turns into a deciduous tree with drooping branches. The child-shadow takes the flask and waters the tree. From very far away, there comes the lamenting of an old woman, but she is not to be seen.

4

Home for Christmas

The seats looked much more like armchairs in the foyer of a luxury
hotel than seats in an ordinary-looking, yellow minibus. There
were just two in each row, no more than eight in total, plus the
driver's seat and the one next to it. A very corpulent man could
lean back comfortably in one of the seats, relax and have a nice
snooze during the trip. There was even space between the seats for
little tables to put coffee or juice on. Altogether an almost homely
atmosphere!

The boy was already in the bus and waiting for his father to get
in and sit beside him, when a woman, who acted as if she knew
him, came and settled down in the next 'armchair' without asking
if anyone else was sitting there. So his father, without complaint, sat
down next to the driver in the seat narrower and less comfortable
than the others.

The woman, who had a pointy nose like a duck, immediately
turned towards him and asked in a particularly loud voice: 'Do you
think we'll get there before midnight? Your father can be as helpless
as a child after a long trip, so I'll have to run about and heat the
house again before putting him to bed.' She leaned towards him
with all her make-up and her astrakhan fur coat, but he, oddly
enough, caught a whiff of wool and cured meat. Moreover, this
cheerful and well-groomed woman from who knows where seemed
to have done herself up and to be about to go out to a carnival.

'Isn't that right, Daddy?' she called out to his father, as the other
passengers were getting in and taking their seats, some of them
getting in each other's way.

'Yes, my love: You're right.'

He didn't even have time to ask himself how his father fitted
into this because the woman kept prattling on: 'Marriage can be

positive thing if it's built on healthy foundations. And we all know who lays the foundations. The woman! Isn't that right, Daddy?'

Fortunately a voice called out – not his father's, but the driver's: 'All in and ready to go?'

'Yes. Let's go!' everyone answered with one voice.

'Well, here's wishing you a good trip,' the woman said, offering him some vacuum packed prunes, pitted and juicy. As he was having his fourth, he thought there was perhaps something good in her excessive openness after all. The fat fellow with a fine moustache sitting behind her gladly accepted some prunes, too.

'I know you from somewhere,' she went on, 'I think I've seen you on television. Oh yes, now I remember, it was the advertisement for Skopsko beer!'

'Oh, that was for a little fee on the side. I'm not a real beer-lover, to be honest – I prefer a drop of good wine,' the man said, gesticulating with his arms in quite an animated way; unusual for a man of his weight. 'Horatio Jingle, actor!'

'You have a funny name, too,' she mumbled, as if she hadn't heard him, and then turned round and looked at him with undisguised interest. 'Yes, yes, that's you. Hey Daddy, that Horatio fellow is with us on the bus. Oh, what was his surname again?'

'Jingle,' the actor repeated amicably.

'So tell me, Horatio: what are the prospects for an actor these days to live off his work?' she said and stared at him while she was waiting for his answer (an especially unpleasant habit), but the fat actor began to explain to her in his calm bass voice, with lively gesticulation:

'Each of us feels at some time that he's hit the bottom.'

It was mostly the woman and Horatio who talked at the beginning of the trip, but later the voices of the other five passengers merged into quite a cacophony (although the woman was still the loudest). His father was the exception, sitting peacefully and quietly near the driver.

* * *

'Half an hour's break!' the driver shouted.

Although he was used to unusual roadside taverns, this one was in a category of its own. There was an improvised bar, which actually looked more like a battered and peeling old lectern lifted from some university storeroom. Above it, in pride of place on the wall, hung a self-made flag made of wrapping paper and held together by a variety of sticky tapes. It bore a sun, a pyramid, and an anvil with hammer and tongs. Photographs cut out of school textbooks had been framed and nailed to the wall next to the flag: mini-portraits of Alexander the Great, Macedonian revolutionaries and the President. On the shelf above the bar lay plastic casks of wine with an imitation-wood finish, and between them were boxes of herb teas – St John's wort, mint, thyme and basil – or at least that's what it said on the side.

The name of this roadhouse was fully in keeping with its appearance; *The Balkan Egyptian Club*, in reference to the local Romanies who believed they had arrived in the region from India via the land of the Pharaohs.

All the tables but two were vacant. At one of them, two men were playing draughts, while two others looked on and commented. The man sitting at the next table didn't look as if he was interested in their game. He just sat there in his unbuttoned grey coat, with a grey-blue striped shirt and white pants with suspenders underneath, a mesh baseball cap on his head, and distractedly sipped his Turkish coffee and smoked. The little bus-load of travellers, with the pointy-nosed woman at the fore (where had his father got to?), descended on the vacant tables.

'Let's sit next to him,' Horatio said. 'May we?'

'Of course, in fact, I'm quite looking forward to a chat with someone from home.'

The waiter came.

'A small "Alexandria" white wine for me and a Cola for the boy,' Horatio said and then prompted the man next to him. 'And you?'

'That's a good idea. Wine for me too, please. They say to stay away from cafés and bars, but today I feel like a bit of company.'

'It looks like we're at the right table then. Hm, let me ask you something: do you know why people touch glasses when they drink wine? To satisfy all the senses. You see its colour, you smell its aroma, and before you take a mouthful you clink glasses. Why? To hear how it sounds!'

'That's a good one!' the fellow shouted and gave a hearty laugh.

'A sick old joke – but good for starting a conversation. So where are you from?'

'From far away, friend. Yesterday morning I set out from Germany, where I work, by noon I was in Slovenia, and now I'm here, and speaking our language again. You have to have some good cheer. To your health!'

After the first few mouthfuls of wine, the fellow really got talking.

'My boss is phenomenal. I don't know how much he earns. A multi-billionaire! But he understands us workers at the same time. Take me, for example: I come home every year for Christmas, although they don't celebrate it at the same time as us with our Orthodox calendar.'

'Yes, when our Jesus is being born, theirs is already crying and laughing and being breastfed. Advanced as he is in the West, perhaps he's already taking his first steps!'

The fellow smiled blankly at Horatio's wisecrack and went on with his own story.

'But my boss agreed. He said: "You've been a good worker all these years. You work overtime without grumbling, so of course you can go home for Christmas. If you work well, I won't say no." And he's a man of his word. He sets you a quota, and if you exceed it there's a bonus. That's all that counts for him – success. Business means profit. That's how my boss is.'

'Sorry to interrupt, but that jars on me. Anyone in the arts and culture in this country has to eke out a living, and here you are talking about filthy lucre.'

'What?'

'Forgive me if the comparison sounds far-fetched, but with pigeons the chief bird spends the whole time chasing the others so they don't peck a crumb, although he goes hungry himself. With people it's the other way round: the boss forces you to work all the time, and he creams off the money.'

'My boss pays me well. I'm sure I earn five or ten times as much as you.'

'That wouldn't surprise me... I guess that's how things are today,' Horatio said to him, but perhaps more to the boy. 'Personal gain has become the main goal of our lives. We all wear masks of compassion, understanding and humility to help us rake in more dough. And inside – poor suckers that we are – we tell ourselves we're something special. Success? What is success after all? Do you consider yourself successful?'

'Yes, I do.'

'I wish I could say that for myself. I used to have my sights set on success. But that's a very fluid category in my profession. One day you're at the top, people recognize you in the street, your photo is everywhere and, what's more important, you're full of self-confidence. But before two or three years have passed, nothing works any more and your former self-importance goes down the plughole. Film-directors shun you or give you demeaning little supporting parts. And you start to whinge and whine: oh, what rotten luck, that's my chances gone, I've got no choice but to make a living from hack roles in this accursed country in this brain-dead age. And although you're as fit as a fiddle you just can't make it, you've got no money for this, you need money for that, you get frustrated and start shouting: "You're all communist blockheads!", although you don't have the faintest idea what communism is. That's a Macedonian actor for you today, and that's why you see me in the beer ads.'

This outburst is like he's rehearsing for his role in an evening performance, the boy fancied. *It's as if he's talking to people who aren't here.* And, sure enough, the initial élan of the conversation evaporated and the fellow slumped back in his chair. Almost in silence, they all finished off their drinks. The simple fellow was the fastest.

'Please let me pay,' Horatio said.

'Out of the question – it's my shout. I'm paying for you and the kid as a thank-you for your company. And now I have to keep driving. They're waiting for me in my home village.'

He shook hands with them as if he was in a hurry, and his cordiality seemed forced. Only when he got up from the table did they notice that he was unhealthily pale in the face, with dark circles around his eyes.

'I feel bad, you know,' Horatio said a little later.

'Why?'

'For unsettling the fellow like that, you know, I think you can say there are several very different groups of people who feel the need to leave this country. The biggest is the diaspora – the economic emigrants. Macedonia has capitulated in the two most significant fields, you know: education and the brain drain, which boils down to the same thing. Either way it's a net loss. People are obliged to leave their home country in search of a better life. *Ubi bene, ibi patria!* What people discuss here every day in the parliaments, newspapers, cafés and even bedrooms is a farce. They call it politics, but it solves no problems and the young people are running away from us, never to come back!' Horatio sighed and drained his wineglass, but his unquenchable thirst for conversation did not allow him to take a break.

'What if...,' the boy ventured to say, but Horatio continued:

'There's also another, much smaller group of Macedonian migrants, who don't stop roaming the world in this age of low wages; and where they need a visa for every damn country. You'd be surprised how many young and mainly poor people from our little country have made it all the way to India, Cuba and China. I don't understand either how they manage to find the means, but somehow they do. Yes, my boy, if you ask me, those are the true wayfarers. The diggers.'

'Diggers? I don't get it...'

'That's right, diggers. The ones who travel in the vertical dimension – downwards and inwards.'

They left *The Balkan Egyptian Club*. The parking lot was not the same. His father, the other passengers and the driver of the minibus were not there. The talkative woman with the pointy nose was gone, and they looked in vain for the minibus. There was just a strange little train in the clearing where the parking lot had been, with an engine and two little carriages.

* * *

The train puffed as it climbed the thickly forested slopes. We were passing a peaceful mountain range with rounded, wooded summits, as green and lush as if it was not almost Christmas but springtime, when the luxuriance of nature is most evident. No one had a camera, but the scenery was absolutely photogenic.

'Just look at these mountains!' Horatio exclaimed. 'They need every bit of a million years to move, you know. And we people beside them – don't we look like the fastest and flightiest of creatures? We're constantly on the move, grab this – then let go of it, so the next thing doesn't run away from you. And your whole life is like that,' he said, ceremonially spreading his arms and raising his eyebrows, a gesture many would call novelettish or old-fashioned, but which suited his character perfectly: 'Run, keep on running, until one day, one hour, one moment you stop, who knows why, perhaps because of the photo you wanted to take from the little train and which by complete chance will fall out of your album, and you'll think, horrified: just look at that child. Why, that was me! So many years of my life have passed irretrievably, and there's no going back.'

The boy listened to Horatio, who now seemed to have become taller and fatter, and he realized he didn't understand all he was saying.

Inside, the carriage wasn't divided into compartments but had rows of forward-facing wooden seats. Children were milling about between them. It was probably some primary-school excursion – fifth or sixth year – because the girls had outgrown the boys, who were bumping into each other and jostling around the girls like drones around queen bees.

* * *

Then they saw a group of men digging beside the track. They were wearing monotonous, faded, grey uniforms, and some of them had on dirty, torn gloves. The children were glued to the windows of the carriage as the little train edged slowly past the workers.

'Who are these sad-looking men?' the boy asked, slightly surprised at his high, childish voice.

'Those are... how should I put it... those are men who have done something bad in their lives and now have to bear the consequences.'

'And their punishment is having to dig like this?'

'That's right, my lad. See those other men at the side, with helmets, who aren't digging but holding rifles and yelling?'

'Yes.'

'Those are the guards. They make sure the convicts don't run away.'

'Do they give them a beating?'

'They don't just give them a beating, but beat them to death. Time ticks away very slowly here. The work is hellishly hard and onerous, and it goes on day after day, from morning till night. The pickaxe is as heavy as lead, the ground is stony, and you long to lie down for a rest, even just for one minute, but no: you have to keep your eyes propped open because the eagle-eyed guards will see you if you falter, and then they'll rush at you with their rifle butts for a bit of sport.'

One of the convicts, with sunken cheeks, raised his eyes towards the little train. The boy noticed the dark bags under his eyes and the sprig of Christmas fir in the breast pocket of his worn-out uniform. Why did that poor, tormented man look like his father?

* * *

'Human physiology is imperfect, laddy.'

'What is physiology?'

'Everything to do with your body. You wake up in the morning after a good night's sleep – rested, fresh, and so on... And then something down below tells you: you need to pee! There's nothing you can do about it. You jump out of bed on the left-hand side, not the right, and your left slipper is missing – pushed under the bed, you suppose – and when you kneel down to look for it you bang your head on the edge of the bed. The pain really wakes you up; you curse and swear, you go to pee, and nothing is left of the good mood from when you woke up. Ah, talking of sleep, I was complaining to one of my sweet girlfriends –," Horatio made a short, dramatic pause to emphasize the plural, *girlfriends*, 'that I'm finding it ever harder to get to sleep when I go to bed in the evening. And do you know what she told me?'

'What?'

'"You can't get to sleep because your age is greater than your shoe size!" Just imagine, laddy, she said that as blunt as a bludgeon, but I didn't let it get me down. The size of my pants is still greater than my age, ha, ha, ha!'

That's because you're fat, he thought and immediately felt embarrassed for being so nasty, and only then, when he looked away from Horatio's face, did he notice that they were no longer travelling in the little train, and the school kids and the convicts and the mountain range were gone.

* * *

One day he would probably say to him: 'I remember you! We were once on a bus together; I remember it well, although it was many years ago. You're an actor and I remember your name, it was something striking... Horatio... Horatio Jingle, that's it! In fact, we met an even longer time ago when I was child, in a little train on a school excursion... Isn't it funny for us to be meeting again like this; I'm a grandpa with three granddaughters, and my son's wife – it's his second marriage – is pregnant, so soon I'll have another. But you... you're still the same, unchanged, with the same moustache... you haven't aged a day!'

'Do you really think so?'

'It's incredible, even your voice is the same. Most characteristic. If you think back over all the times we've spoken, I've had three different voices – a child's, a young man's and now, how should I put it, a rather mature man's. Your name's Horatio Jingle, right?'

'Yes.'

At this muted response, he would probably feel the urge to scratch himself on the head as if he had dandruff, although he would only have a little patch of hair left on the back of his head. But Horatio's face would melt into that familiar, broad smile, and he would say: 'Cheer up, what's there to be glum about? And if we've known each other for so long there's no need to be awkward.'

'I thought I'd made a mistake... it's getting dark already... I can't see all that well with these glasses, so perhaps I ought to be heading home.'

'Don't be afraid, lad, there are no terrorists or robbers here.'

'But where are we exactly, Mr Horatio?' he would ask, but by some strange twist of fate he would be gone again. 'What's happening to me? Just a moment ago, we were together, and now suddenly he vanishes. Everything can be so different to what I expect. It's as if I'm living in an express dream. First the present, then the past, and next what? Going by my age, this must be some time in the future.'

* * *

There, in the future, he would meet face to face with his loneliness in a landscape like a Hollywood adaptation of a fairy tale, with elaborately staged artificial illumination from spotlights: the night would be arrested in its coming just enough to reveal the contours of the many-branched bushes of white and red roses, among which amber eyes (of black cats or werewolves?) flashed, and he would wander lost along the village path with a layer of thick, dry dust, so that clouds rose with his every step.

'You st-u-u-upid old fart,' he would hear a voice like a netherworldly whisper. He would see a shapeless spectre and immediately feel its deathly cold breath beneath a slate-grey, musty cloak covering the spectre's head and hazy body; only its outstretched right hand would beckon him to follow. And despite the terrible fear that made him freeze from head to toe, he would follow the spectre unwillingly, like a captive soul. The village path, half-visible in the pale, synthetic light of the moon, would lead to the cemetery, where tall silhouettes of crosses and monuments leaning in the sickly soil froze his petrified body even more. The spectre would slip silently through the half-open cemetery gate.

He too would squeeze through, staggering as he went. The spectre would stop and, with its long, bony finger, point to the inscription on a derelict tombstone. He would read his own name there.

'No, no!' he would stammer, as an uncontrollable tremor began to seize his lower jaw.

'You will rot in the grave,' he would hear that chilling whisper again.

But then, amidst that madness, a huge, shaggy creature would emerge from the darkness and come shambling towards him on its hind legs, growling and extending its gruesome claws. This would be too much for him. He would start to scream and break into a run, stumbling as he tried to get as far as possible from that terrible place. And when his squeals of fear were interrupted by an unseen hand (please not that of the spectre!) forcing him to turn round, he would see the ghostly bear strike the hideous spectre with its paw; the apparition would collapse from that single blow and vanish the next instant. He would turn again and continue to run, but the bear would call out: 'Stop, my son, it's me!' He would recognize his voice, stop running and wait for him. The bear would come up to him, large and panting, but not as huge as he had first thought. The bearskin would fall away to reveal his father, who now stood before him, handsome and elegantly dressed as always. Hardly would they be reunited when a third figure would come bumbling along, and who could it be but Horatio, who would tell him in his charming bass voice: 'You know what it says in the Bible – if you have faith, even as small as a mustard seed, you can move mountains.'

He would feel a light as a feather, as happy as an angel, as exuberant as a first-grader. And in that optimistic mood he would hear the ringing of the church bells.

'What day is it today?'

'Christmas!' his father and Horatio would answer in unison.

* * *

While he was hugging his father, and crying and giggling at the same time, he woke up. For a while – quite a long while – he was completely disoriented and gaped at the ceiling (what day is it? where am I? how old am I?), and then he slowly looked The bed was his and the room was his. A fresh May breeze through the open window. 'What a mix-up! I never had a dream like that before,' he thought as he went to the window to take in a few deep breaths. Still not quite awake, he stared at verdant Mount Vodno, which the clear air seemed to bring right up close to the city.

All of a sudden, he realized he had to be at the bus station by noon. His bus was leaving at 12.15pm. It was not a real bus, he remembered, but a minibus they would be travelling in, the friendly travel-agency lady had told him. A nice, modern European one.

Minibus? He scratched his shaggy hair. *That sounds strangely familiar*, and scratching his head again, he started for the bathroom to have his morning wash.

Marko's Little Sister

Marko was three years old when his younger sister was born, on New Year's Eve. While his father was taking his mother to hospital, Marko found some string and tied together the kitchen table and the chairs; he also tied the Christmas tree to the legs of his little bed. His parents found this hilarious, and whenever they told the story to friends they couldn't stop laughing.

Two years later, Marko's mother had to go into hospital again, this time because of 'problems down below'. By coincidence, it was exactly before the New Year's break. So the children wouldn't be unsettled, their mother made the traditional family roast turkey stuffed with liver, apple and prunes. The operation went well, thank God, and on 31st December their father, who went to see her every day, took her a nicely packaged piece of the turkey on her favourite plate with the yellow flower-pattern. The children stayed alone at home to play. When their father came back from the hospital, from the front door he heard Marko's little sister crying fitfully. He rushed inside, and there was a sight to see: Marko was dragging his sister through the house with a cord around her neck.

Later, his parents decided to get rid of all the string, cord and rope in the house – secretly, so as not to anger their son. And this they did, but Marko soon became anxious, started to search and to pick through all the drawers, and then openly to demand string from his parents. 'If there isn't any, buy some for me!' he yelled at them. They made up an excuse: they hadn't been able to buy any string or rope because the shops had run out. Marko threw a mighty tantrum lasting several days, and then he suddenly calmed down and stopped asking for string.

The next New Year was drawing near. The family lived in a house with a garden, and although the father was no gardener, the unpruned bushes and straggly trees provided a welcome little refuge of calm when things inside got too noisy or hectic.

The tallest of the trees was a pine, and the father decided to decorate it with little lanterns and other yuletide ornaments to please the children. He got up on a stool and had started hanging up the decorations, when a glance through the window of the children's room showed Marko lying limp on the carpet, with a string around his neck fastened to the bars of his sister's cot. *Where did he get it from?* the father managed to ask himself, although he immediately felt ashamed at the thought. He ran into the room, and there Marko lay stock-still on the floor with his eyes closed, although visibly still breathing. The father acted as if nothing had happened, tiptoed back out of the room and put his finger to his lips to tell the others to be quiet. Marko stayed lying on the carpet for some time longer, then grumpily got up, untied the rope and stuck it in a drawer.

Many years later, Marko's sister, now a young woman, dreamed that someone was in her flat. A shadow. She went out into the hall and in the darkness she brushed against a coarse woollen jumper that seemed to be made of string or some other rough fibre. Then, in her dream, she tried to call out: 'Marko, I love you!' and woke up screaming and covered in sweat. In the morning, her husband told her she had yelled: 'Marko, cold and blue!' Perhaps her tongue had got twisted, as sometimes happens in dreams.

Her dream occurred at Christmas, just before her birthday and one year after the tragic death of her brother.

This fairy tale should not be told
while leafing through women's magazines

The Huntsman

We know that the pain your own people inflict on you cannot be
quieted unless you make strangers of them or yourself; it is not the
despised, but the forgotten man who is miserable.

CHRISTA WOLF, *Cassandra*

The smell of the forest – the smell of gunpowder – and the calm certainty of death. How exciting it is! You lie in wait for the animal and together with it you become part of nature, part of the One. You are connected inextricably by the shot. The animal itself then begins to understand you. A strong emotional bond, even a kind of love, is forged between you. The animal says: 'I am imbued in the pupil of your eye and the sight of your rifle. I have come here for you to find me and free me.' All is quiet, the sunrise illuminates the forest clearing and you can hear it breathing, as if you were at the border between two kingdoms, the earthly and the supernatural. You pull the trigger.

Therein lies the beauty of the hunt, in that cycle of life and death. I have been given the role of the hunter, the deer is my prey, and when the chase begins it is as if we are alone in the expanse of the forest. Once you feel the might of the forest you never forget it. Many are scared to the marrow by it and find every encounter with it horrendous; they think there is a beast ready to pounce in every thicket, and every rustling is a werewolf. But there are also those who fall in love with the forest forever, with all its different trees and shadows, denizens and sounds. The forest is my domain. It sharpened my senses and allowed me to run fast for a long time if I have to, to skilfully climb high branches, to wade a river or swim across a mountain lake, however cold. For me there is no prey too fast or too strong – nothing is uncatchable – be it rabbit or bear, wild goose or boar. I have a solution for all of them so I can add them to my collection of trophies!

My only regret is that I haven't been able to hunt rhinoceroses; they say their horns can make you really rich, because they are ground up and used to make aphrodisiacs, which apparently fetch millions. But although Africa is rich in game, it is far away. I am a man of these climes and my quarry is here.

I am a hunter by nature, just as I am naturally a loner. I am happy to be by myself in all weathers, fair and foul. Or at least that's what thought until I met her. Even when I was with a woman, I never stayed in the relationship for long – a week or two at most – and that was mainly in the winter months, when the urge drives hunters, just as it does wolves and foxes, to seek a mate. I always found it ridiculous whenever I heard one of those summertime romances, because in July and August I'm too busy to scratch myself and chasing after women is furthest from my mind. If I chase anything, it's animals: I'm constantly at their heels, and you need to save up your energy for that labour, not fritter it away!

That's how I was until I met her.

Like I say, I'm not particularly fond of ceremonies, weddings and other mass events, but my position as 'royal huntsman' meant that I had to report to the court once a week. Back then, the country was ruled by a king. I entered his service when he was already a widower, forlorn and rather too absent-minded for a king. He preferred the fresh, cool air to the heated chambers of the palace, although it is one of the stateliest in this part of the world. Wearing dungarees and a faded XXL T-shirt which was tucked into his pants, over his pot belly and hanging out at the back, he spent all day in the gardens between the fruit trees and the tomatoes, and there he received me. He would distractedly listen to my report on the state of the royal forests and hunting grounds while pruning the roses, or digging, or sitting on a wooden stool. Occasionally he asked me to tell him a story from nature. He listened to me just as distractedly as when I delivered my report, and I even imagined he wasn't there at all, but I was mistaken: 'The bit about the hare is interesting,' he said (I had told him that a hare twitches its nose all the time, both when it's feeding and when it's resting). 'It wiggles its nose all the time, you say. Oh, consciousness... it's still there even when our brain seems to be inactive,' he would remark quietly, without looking at me. Although I naturally couldn't agree with his opinion because my brain works all the time when I'm hunting, I was glad he took an interest in my stories, in his absent-minded way. Later, when I was seeing the queen, and especially after his death, I sometimes thought he had also been awkward and lost when dealing with her – his second, passionate and dangerous wife – and that therefore he must have been unhappy. But those were cursory thoughts because I myself was 'gone with the wind' when this woman held me clenched between her hot thighs and her arrogant, ambitious mind.

Terrible, truly terrible was the power she wielded over me! Previously, everything had been based on simple logic for me. One plus one is two. One minus one is zero. An animal. A shot. My prize. The forest. Sunrise. Sunset. I am a hunter, I sleep by the campfire in a glade; the howling of wolves comes from away somewhere, and that's just one of the woodland lullabies I doze off to, but my sleep is not careless; my rifle is by my side, my finger on the trigger just in case, although when I wake up in the morning the fire is still crackling and the wolves are long since gone.

But when she fused me to her with a hundred searing magnets I was no longer the same. When the paw of a large bear comes down on you, regardless of whether it's an angry swipe or a friendly tap, you end up with a wound. My heart-rending love for her was like the paw of that bear! As soon as I woke up in the forest, I would be assailed by thoughts of how to get to her in the palace as quickly as possible. What should I bring her as a present today? Deerskin slippers? A rabbit-tail muff to warm her ears? Bear lard to make compresses for her neck and face, to smooth out wrinkles? If I was fortunate enough to be allowed to spend the night in her chamber, even as I was stealing out of the palace in the morning without being seen and vaulted over the spiked fence (at least that bit was easy enough), I was already planning how to see her again as soon as possible. That's what you call possessed. Even when the morning was sunny and peaceful, the sky in me was rent by lightning and all my inner storms and wellsprings were tied to just one thought: when would I be with her again? I was so intoxicated with love and mad about her. And her – oh, how she toyed with me! For entertainment, she made me chew and swallow the flowers of the fresh posies I picked for her in the forest meadows. Or she would order me to be a dachshund for the day and bring her her slippers in my teeth and eat from a plate on the floor, without using my hands.

But I didn't yet know her when I was having those passive conversations with the king about tomatoes and hares, so I couldn't have dreamed what would become of me. Like I say, I was completely different back then: free of everything superfluous, oriented solely towards the hunt. Sometimes his daughter, Snow White, would come out and join us in the garden. A girl of white and pink, with a cute strawberry mouth and eyes large and moist like a fawn's: as pure in her heart as the forest dew on pine needles. These days, when my memories are swirling in a wild vortex and I happen to think of little Snow White, I feel a tide of calm come over me, and a smile returns to my face. She was as gentle as a dove, but frolicsome and much more inquisitive than her father. There was no keeping her still; she would skip along and ask me question after question: 'Why do woodpeckers eat hazelnuts, Mr Hunter?', 'Why do people say someone is "lynx-eyed"?', 'Why do bears have to sleep during the winter?' 'Does a blackbird always sing at half past four in the morning?' Or, sitting cross-legged on the low stone wall in the garden, she would sing some of her own little songs with a clear, resonant voice, her head raised and eyes lively, as if she could already talk to her woodland friends, the birds and nimble-footed fairies.

How could the queen, in spite of her distorted mind, think I was perverted enough to be able to harm such a tender, lovely human being? Did she think I was a gormless redneck who made no distinction between a girl and a wild piglet or a rabbit? What a depraved, evil heart! But then again, did I not behave in front of her like a mute, a servile gladiator prepared for any sacrifice for the sake of his mistress? She had terrible power over me from that very day at noon, in the garden, where the king listened distractedly to my reports, and introduced me to his new queen. It surprised me to see her with the king, there between the tomato seed-plots, rather than finding him alone or with Snow White. I had heard from the fat-bottomed, gossiping maidservants that the king was completely befuddled by the new queen, that she had wrapped him around her little finger from day one, and that he trembled at her every word. I admit I thought that sounded ridiculous, and I imagined her as a bony sorceress with a teased-up hairdo, shrieking as she chased the plump, troubled king through the chambers of the palace. But what I saw was completely different: the body of the woman who stood before me, although clad in an orange cotton dress, gave the impression of being naked. Only Spanish women have such irresistible, unconcealed beauty, from what I've heard, although I had never seen it before setting eyes on her. Long-necked and fair-skinned, with breasts that danced to the slightest movement, she had lush, raven-black hair plaited into a sumptuous chignon. Her voice, too, was completely different to what I expected – a self-possessed, almost soft alto. And when I bowed to show my respect, her dark eyes, calm but with flint glass in their depths, looked at me condescendingly and calculatingly as if I was a slave on sale at the market; her stare was inquisitorial, yet it throbbed at the same time with the assertiveness of a cougar on heat.

I spent the afternoon following our first meeting in the forest, as usual, and my keen senses could make out animals' territory markings, as usual, but not only was I unable to hunt, but I couldn't even move. It was as if a stone had fallen from the sky and hammered me into the ground. A hitherto unknown feeling of emptiness, accompanied by senseless heart-racing, held me in a vice, and when the birds started returning to their nests I was still there, sitting on a tree stump and struggling with a dry bitterness in my throat. I had changed beyond recognition. She already contr me through the magic power of absence. The spring air was by a multitude of stars, and their bright rays seemed to pierce me right in the chest, producing a dull, sickly yearning. The quick, clear murmur of the stream, that life-giving sound that used to stir me and fill me with zest and energy, now cast me into an uneasy slumber, a fruitless torpor, and I could only stare straight ahead, without seeing or noticing anything.

Just as the landscape, in which my skilled hunter's eye used to detect the tiniest detail, had vanished before my eyes, so too the space in my head had gone blank, and only one thought, if it can be called a thought, revolved there monotonously: *I have to see her again! I have to see her again!*

I rose together with the early birds, which flew out from their nests, and was at the palace again at daybreak. The king, poor little fellow began to develop heart problems around that time, and his medication made him sleep a lot. Although I greatly wished the queen would be awake, I didn't dare to hope; but she was up, out on the terrace in a dark blue tracksuit. I saw her squatting with her hands on the ground in front of her, as if she was about to polish the shiny marble tiles. Then she spread her thighs and, seemingly without effort, lifted her lovely bottom and legs off the ground, and there she remained on just her hands, with a resolutely stretched neck and her sharp chin thrust forwards. She looked like an enormous locust (but much more attractive than Marquis de Saint-Crookstile, who I'll come to later). She called that position a 'magpie', as I was soon to find out, and her outspread fingers and the prominent network of veins on her hands were eerily remini-scent of a magpie's talon. She remained in that amazing position for almost a minute then calmly lowered herself to the floor and lay down on her stomach. Soon she began to lift first of all her head, then the upper part of her body, and with a radiant face she raised her torso until it was at right angles to her legs on the ground, and then she stopped. All of a sudden, her lower row of immaculately white teeth flashed, and from between them came an abrupt hiss – 'ssss' – which continued as she lowered her head and body to the ground and only stopped when she was calmly lying on her stomach again (she so much resembled a snake, with almost innate, unconscious movements). Her eyes were closed as she did these exercises and exhibited all the details of her perfect figure like an actress on stage, yet I felt she knew I was nearby and she seemed to be sneering inside at the dismay of a gawping idiot. The master of the situation lurked beneath her closed eyelids, and her expression acquired a terrible weight even without looking at me. She had captivated me with that gaze at our first meeting, and now she just needed to pull the strings.

Later, when I got to know her, I realized this was her regular morning yoga-ritual. The positions, called 'asanas', many of which were named after animals – lion, cat, pigeon, peacock, tortoise, rooster, fish and frog – became the basis of one of her games with me. She would take up position in one of the asanas, and in that incredible pose she would ask me: 'And what is this?' That outwardly childish game of hers would have been endearing if she had remained a child in it. But she took pleasure in tormenting me. 'If you guess right, you can mount me. If you get it wrong, you're banned from the palace for three days!' That's how she was, clever and cruel.

When I took Snow White into the forest, ostensibly to carry out the queen's command, her little dress fluttered and billowed around her knees from our running; she ran without effort and peered wide-eyed into every thicket as we went, bent over to smell the flowers, registered the chirps of the birds, and asked me her usual questions: 'Look at that one hopping along the ground. Is it a wren? What a big nest that female nightingale has. And there comes the male – he's bringing her worms.'

She was already fifteen, and the exhilarated little girl whose mouth used to gape in awe had now turned into a real beauty, inwardly just as effusive and simple-hearted as before, but physically mature and endowed with the curvaceousness of a grown woman. It made me think how many long years I had been under the power of the queen, how long she had made me submit to her – all just for a moment of bliss – and how long she had exploited me... but now things would be different!

I had made the plan long in advance. The hardest part was pretending I would leave Snow White alone in the forest. Nevertheless, it was heart-wrenching when she begged me not to leave her at the mercy of the night and the wild animals. Although everything had been arranged, like I say, I had to pay "the Seven" amply so they would take Snow White into their hut and look after her.

I made the deal with Doc and his midgety brothers. I had been on cash-in-hand terms with the dwarves for years. As well as mining ore, they earned their livelihood in several other ways, too. They always complained what a struggle it was to earn a crust, but in fact they were crafty hypocrites who deposited their accumulated riches in foreign banks every month. I myself used to trade in subterranean fungi from the titches, which they alone knew where to find in the depths of the forest. Those fungi were highly prized and more valuable than truffles, so Doc, Grumpy and the others made me pay half a fortune for their services. But I wasn't naïve either, and, pretending the fungi were a secret aphrodisiac, I peddled them to rich, aging courtiers, flaccid dukes and bewigged princes, who spared no expense to acquire unnatural, erotic powers. I earned as much money from their ridiculous wish to be fornicators at the age of one hundred as if I had been selling powdered rhinoceros horn! My best client was in fact Marquis de Saint-Crookstile, whom I mentioned earlier, the king's counsellor – a boring count of about seventy-five, who blatantly gossiped about others, while knowing that no one ever dared to gossip about him. While the king was still alive, this spineless fellow devoted all his time, apart from that spent on denunciations, on courting the young maidservants, and afterward he boasted about having deflowered them. (They, in turn, knew all about the old lecher's passions and played the role of seduced village virgins most convincingly, with tears in their eyes and smeared lamb's blood between their legs.) Saint-Crookstile became the main organizer of the balls at the palace almost every second night, when the courtiers and their escorts, all powdered and prettied up, crowded the Central Hall and the music blared until the early hours.

But enough of me going on about that old rake; although it's true he hated my guts, he did pay me the best rate for the fungi. At first, I saved the money from selling it to make sure I had the best gun and sights, but after the queen bewitched me I began spending it on presents for her. I, who until then had never dreamed of going into a shop, wasted whole evenings trawling Cavalli, Ungaro, Max Mara, Dolce & Gabbana boutiques and other stores with macaroni names, constantly fearing I'd choose the wrong piece of apparel among the dressed up dummies and overflowing shelves. She would write down for me on a small piece of paper: 'A suit with close-fitting blazer and a skirt coming down to a little above the knees, ending abruptly with frills at about boot-height' or 'a short jacket of light-coloured tweed with gold braid and ethno-ornamentation, to be worn together with a fanciful leopard-print skirt edged with a pale lace band'. Who can understand such cryptic stuff? Certainly not me, as I staggered, tormented and flustered, through that ordered, rich and alien world of fashion; my stomach tensed up and I always felt under pressure to make the right choice. Besides, she was never satisfied.

But over those last few years I began to save again. Who knows why – it was another big change – but I put part of the money aside, and after a while I had a pretty packet, which certainly came in handy when I needed to pay "the Seven" for helping out with Snow White. But I really hadn't expected that the queen would come up with what she did.

It was all to do with her obsession with the Magic Mirror. She spent more time with it than with all the kings, hunters and other men of this world put together. In front of it, she was in her element: doubled, albeit in mirror image, as if she had painted a self-portrait every morning. The mirror was the only thing she obeyed unconditionally. At times she accepted the whispered counsels of the slimy Marquis de Saint-Crookstile, especially when it was a matter of organizing a particularly lavish ball, emptying the court's coffers or doubling taxes, although most times he would curl up like a swatted insect (he resembled a locust anyway) in the face of her calm, deadly alto. But the mirror, which she had brought in her dowry chest in a specially locked, lead-sheathed coach, was like her own, private deity. She believed everything it told her, and the morning when its omniscient voice declared that

Snow White was more beautiful than her was definitely the worst morning of her life. Or rather, one of the two worst, the other being when it told her that Snow White was still alive.

Once more, it was that senile snake Saint-Crookstile who revealed Snow White's hiding place to the queen (how could he have found out if not from one of "the Seven" shrimps – for good money, of course). Without saying a word to me, the queen secretly turned herself into a wrinkled witch, hobbled with the steps of an old hag to the hut and poisoned Snow White. I have no doubt that wretched Saint-Crookstile told her the way there and when the girl would be alone. Only when the deed was done, after she returned, did the queen invite me to the palace.

'Come in. The door was always open for you *until now* – except for three days whenever you got the asana wrong,' she said.

I could tell there was an ominous snarl creeping up behind her outwardly calm voice: '*Until now*, that is. As of today, you are never to set foot in this palace again!'

She announced in that same cold, menacing tone that Snow White was dead and that I, too, was as good as dead for her, or rather that she never wanted to see me again in her bed, in the palace, or anywhere in the kingdom.

To put it bluntly, she chased me away; without pardon. 'There is no beauty in force,' she told me and ordered the guards to take me away, beyond the borders of the land. Within just a few hours I went from being the queen's lover and royal huntsman to an exile and vagabond. She took away what I couldn't live without – the forests!

When I look back on that now, after some time has passed, a lump still comes to my throat like a swelling stream, but at least I have the satisfaction – and no so small one at that – of having saved Snow White. I had a plan and I put it into practice. Knowing the queen, I was afraid that she, with malevolent and persistent servants like the mirror and Saint-Crookstile, might find out that the girl was not dead. And that, unfortunately, is exactly what happened. Just so as to be on the safe side, in case something should happen to Snow White, I had given Doc & Co a phial of panacea. It was brewed after a secret old hunter's recipe, which I can only reveal a few ingredients of so as not to detract from the truth of this story; for example, it contained the soft skin of an axolotl, the four-legged fish; a wild bees' honeycomb; the throats of garden snails; the beak of a partridge, and many, many other things I have good reason to keep secret, and which are mixed in precise quantity and proportion, ground, and kept in a cold place for thirty-three days. The antidote is reliable, although one should bear the side effects in mind: the drinker falls into a long, deep sleep, almost without breathing, and can only be woken by the kiss of an enamoured person of the opposite sex.

I took care of that too – I found Snow White a boyfriend. Perhaps 'boyfriend' isn't quite the right word for that young man, but apart from his slightly unusual appearance he was a good match: he was very well situated, being a prince of the Kingdom of Drakula, and, best of all, he had an obvious passion I know so well from my own experience – the passion of love! Young women actually like a certain starkness in a male's appearance, like he had, and the nonchalance in the prince's intense, dark gaze was uncannily combined with a strangely mocking air (perhaps owing to his dark family history), so that when he smiled in his sarcastic way with just the ends of his lips, his eye teeth, which are slightly longer than ordinary, would stand out. I knew the story of the sleeping princess in a glass coffin would excite him.

The antidote worked just as I expected: Snow White fell into a deep, deep sleep, with imperceptible, almost yoga-like breathing (like the queen used to practice so as to slow down the aging of the body's cells). She glowed with the vibrancy of a beautiful plant, alive but motionless, her eyes closed, whether it was light or dark outside. "The Seven" acted the bereaved family very convincingly (the shorter the man, the better the actor!), for which I paid them the last penny of my savings. Kneeling around the coffin with caps in hand, which showed up their baldness and gave the scene a more poignant air, they turned on the waterworks and wailed. 'The Grave of Snow White the Fair' almost became a cult location, and busybodies came in droves from the most distant lands: pilgrims, adventurers and sentimentalists. One morning, among that whole mob of gapers, *he* came riding up on a white stallion with a black star on its forehead, and with an inappropriately long cloak waving behind him, which nevertheless suited him in a way. He towered over her, and everything all around seemed just right – the full white blossoms of the plum trees, the gaudy butterflies chasing each other, and a spider strolling along its thread between the lilies – and he kissed her. I was not in the first rows of the audience, and the bobbing of the heads in front of me prevented me from seeing the kiss scene in detail. In any case, Snow White, who at first was surprised, soon found her bearings in the new situation, and the kissing continued.

Since then I haven't seen Snow White very often, only once or twice a year. She looks rather pale (but I don't know if I've mentioned that she always was a bit anaemic, so her name suited her very well). I asked if she was happy and she answered 'almost', and I'm not certain, but I felt her lips gave a twitch. Oh well, there's a worm in every apple, as the old folk say.

I survived the worst of ordeals with the queen. 'There is no beauty in force,' she told me and cold-heartedly kicked me out. And just let anyone say I didn't do everything for her! I devoted my life to her and her satisfaction, with a love unbearable for the body and agonizing for the soul. And what did she do in return? She laughed at me behind my back to her so-called ladies-in-waiting, those slimy sycophants. I heard that she compared me with a hobbit, a hillbilly with dirt under his fingernails. The ladies of the court giggled loudly and hypocritically. But they're women, and in front of her they pretended to be genteel: 'How are you, Mr Hunter? It's sure been a while since you've come to see Her Majesty, etc., etc.' But in the halls they stuck out their bottoms and waggled their breasts at me. I know that Saint-Crookstile too gossiped in the corridors, calling me a savage from the backwoods, and after the queen chased me away he boasted to anyone who would listen that he – ha, ha – had been the key to them 'getting rid of that Neanderthal'. But his pride was short-lived. His laughter died in his throat when she, in that same cold, resolute voice, relieved him of his position with immediate effect due to his 'constant intrigues at court' and had him deported to the most distant mountain monastery (I can just imagine him in an austere cell, bathed in sweat from the constant howling of a pack of mountain wolves).

But she's not going to get away with it quite so easily after all she did to me. No chance! My few companions, a handful of hunters, always praised me that my fireside stories in the forest were the best they'd heard in all their life. Hunters' tall tales are one thing; I'm sure you've heard people mock us for our share of exaggerations and lies. But everyone pricks up their ears when I tell my tale.

Now I've made up my mind: I'm going to tell the truth about her, with all the frightful and delicate details. *The master of patience bags the best catch*, as we huntsmen say. I'll make this a story about her – not about the feminine, well-built and haughty queen who wraps hare-brained hunters around her little finger, but about the stepmother terrified about aging, while lovely Snow White grows up in front of her, as white as snow, as red as blood, and with glossy hair like ebony, and who becomes more and more beautiful with every passing night. I'll write about the jealous, spiteful queen, who cannot accept the smallest wrinkle on her face when she sees it in the mirror and bathes in fresh mare's milk three times a day and rubs her body with rare herbal elixirs imported from the Far East, while unemployment and penury ravage the kingdom. And talk about spite: she even paid the highest price a woman can pay by turning herself into an old woman, just so as to trick Snow White into taking a bite of the poisoned apple. Knowing the extent of my obsession with her, she had wanted to use me to kill her underage stepdaughter. In the depths of my self-deception, I thought I had met a woman whom, for the first time in my life, I could tell my dreams to, and who would listen and understand. But she, my chosen and worshipped one, was my cold-blooded tormenter!

I've learnt one lesson: that even the most self-assured of us can become weak and helpless and can go from hunter to hunted. He, who was once master of the situation, begins to feel the horrible fear of a hunted animal; it's a feeling he used to consider just part of the game, but now his heart beats like a big, crazy ball that fear kicks through a narrow space without an exit, even without windows, and there's nothing else but the mad beating of the ball – that clod trapped between the walls of his chest. There's a saying among us hunters, 'be healthy as long as you live', which means: be tough, be resistant to minor human illnesses and weaknesses of body and mind because you're a hunter! That's what I was, a hunter and a roamer, made for the forests and nights under the open sky, not for palaces and royal finery. Why did I change so much? I used to wear my heart on my sleeve. You just needed to look me in the face, and it said everything. Now, thanks to her, I'd learnt to act, to disguise the most improper intentions with a smile. I was trapped in myself, a victim of my own powerlessness. I felt I was dying because nothing mattered to me any more, but despair made me more resilient and hard-boiled. Saving Snow White was as much the result of my will as it was of my prudence. I have to continue on my path through the night alone, without losing my way.

So I'm going to tell this tale out of spite, and to fulfil my desire for revenge. At least I derived some benefit from her constant disparagements – I learnt to write! She insulted me by calling me a bumpkin, a hard-bodied animal good for just one thing: for giving her satisfaction in bed. But I, from the naïve desire to please her and make her happy, secretly learnt to write: Painstakingly, but patiently. Proud of my progress, I wrote her a letter, which I think went something like this: 'My one and only love, I swear to you that I will love you for as long as I live – more than the hunt, more than the forest. I need nothing other than you to hold me to your heart. For me, that is the greatest freedom,' and so on, in that vein.

'Great snakes!' she scoffed with her usual sarcasm, blatantly showing that she didn't appreciate my efforts in the slightest. 'If you think basic literacy makes you a clever-dick, then go ahead with your little ego-trip. But we both know that's nothing. And if you've got it into your head to compare me with your festering forest, why don't you talk about yourself – once a stump, always a stump!'

That was one of her typical insults, which I felt I was forgetting, however hurtful they were, because my love was stronger than my memory. But now, when they come back to me as fresh as a buffalo's morning dollops, I'm simply disgusted at everything that woman did to me. She, the outwardly decent and sober queen, who used to thrash about in bed like a bitch on heat, was despotic by nature and could not resist thinking up ever-newer demands for her slave.

Wolves die when they come down with rabies, but foxes pull through without any great detriment. I gazed at her like an infected wolf, stricken with the frenzy of love: she, the foxy one, just had to waggle her tail for me to lose my head and rush off after her without thinking. I was infected with the forlornness and frenzy of love, like rabies, and she would have left me to die in a ditch without the slightest guilty conscience. But I pulled through. There's light at the end of the tunnel. Some time later, maybe it was several months, my desire to hunt again returned. One morning – it's no surprise that all new things begin in the morning – I set off into the forest with my rifle over my shoulder. Not as the royal huntsman now, but as a poacher. Yet the satisfaction was the same, or even greater, because I was doing something I like the most, even if it was forbidden. Although at the beginning I felt I had become a little rusty (I was slow and ham-fisted and kept missing my target) I gradually regained my form. By evening I had bagged two hares and four partridges and killed a fat wild boar. I hit it right between the eyes and it fell like a stone.

The smell of the forest – the smell of gunpowder – and the calm certainty of death. How exciting it is!

The Story of the Letter Q

There once was a king who was unhappy in his marriage and disillusioned with love in general. Such was his exasperation at all the quibbles of his queen, whose name was Quince, that one day he blew a fuse and decreed that the letter Q be abolished – even the 'kw' sound itself – and that it be replaced with 'tw'. Throughout the kingdom, it was now forbidden to say or write 'question': it had to be 'twestion'. 'Query' was to become 'twery'. Instead of 'quintessence' people could only say and write 'twintessence', and 'quail' was to be 'twail'. Such was the depth of the king's disillusionment that the decree even ordered that names containing the letter Q be changed forthwith: 'Quentin' was to be 'Twentin', and 'Quinta' – 'Twinta'. Breaches of the new rules were reported without qualms (sorry, twalms). Soon they mounted, and the fines were nothing to be sneezed at (which had the side effect of augmenting the budget). And so the citizens who were used to being obedient bit their tongues and submitted to the king's decree. Everyone, in fact, except the children.

It must be said that children often don't understand adults, and vice versa. As such, although the decree only applied in a handful of cases (as not many words contain Q), it struck the children as being a bad idea. Or a 'crackpot notion', as their parents used to whisper. The children who followed their parents' conversations were of the same mind, though not because of 'quintessence' (a term they didn't yet understand) or 'inquisitiveness' (an innate characteristic of children, albeit hard to pronounce), but above all because of the names!

Children are often given nicknames by other family members or their playmates, to help identify them. Sometimes these are derived from their name: Quirina becomes Rina, and Quasimodo – Modie. Sometimes nickname are based on an imagined similarity with animals, for example Mousey, Piggy or Bugs Bunny, and other times on a prominent feature of physiognomy – Big-Nose, Jug-Ears, Googly-Eyes. The decree about replacing Q with tw made things awkward for Quentin, Quinta, Quincy and Quartz, who had already suffered due to being given a fancy name by their parents, so being turned into Twentin, Twinta, Twincy and Twartz overnight made each of them feel their hard-won identity was being tampered with. Plus it was unfair, because Peter, Robert, Igor, Irina, Sandra, Andrea and the other children didn't have to change their names at all.

And so a small group of disenfranchised children had no choice (because their parents, like I said, were pusillanimous) but to turn for help to the White Hermit, who lived beyond the edge of the city, in a cabin in the woods.

By common opinion of the adults, the White Hermit was a 'renegade'. Various stories were in circulation concerning his past and why he left to live in solitude. Some claimed he was a member of the royal family who, in the name of ordinary citizens and their empty pockets, had constantly demanded a reduction in the large bills for electricity, heating and water, and was therefore chased away from the court. Others said he had been a leader of the republican opposition who, after a long and tenacious struggle for human rights, became disillusioned with his fellow party members and supposedly like-minded people, who bandied around slogans about justice and equality but were actually filling their foreign bank accounts. Whatever the truth was, many wronged citizens still called on the White Hermit in his cabin to complain and possibly receive some kind of moral support. So it was that Twentin, Twinta, Twinn, Twincy and the other children whose names had been changed knocked on the White Hermit's door one day.

He listened to their grievances and after brief but intense reflection he said to them: 'Let's write directly to the king!' And the White Hermit and the children sat down to write a letter. When they had finished, it read like this:

Our esteemed King, Your Majesty,

Your decree that 'Q(u)' be changed to 'Tw' was certainly issued for a deep and important reason. You, as the most powerful man in our kingdom, can change a thousand things with just one word, and the change of one letter has changed our lives. Although our parents say that tomorrow everything will be better, we don't believe it, because when we go out to play in the street we are met with jeers from the other children and they make us feel ashamed. We sincerely and respectfully request you to take action to give the letter Q back to our names.

They sent the letter to the king the usual way, by post. The court security service checked to see everything was in order and then laid the letter on the king's desk. In the meantime, however, the king had fallen in love again and had difficulty remembering the decree. Even as he was reading the letter he was rather astonished and found it all hard to believe.

He decided to revoke the decree, but just as he was about to sign a new decree annulling the old one his secretary announced that his new bride-to-be had arrived at the palace. The king dropped everything, literally, including the fountain pen for adding his signature, which the children were waiting for so impatiently.

How long would they have to wait? Let us hope not for long. And may the king still be happily in love with his new queen, though perhaps a tiny bit less than in the first flush of love so he will again have time for things at his desk.

This fairy tale should not be told while waiting at
the dentist's to have your false teeth checked

Neverland

I believe it was the great, erudite Cicero who said: *Praeteria mutare non possumus.* We cannot change the past. Where then does this constant need of some human beings come from to resurrect and embellish the past? Do they wish to flee from the problems of the present? That would seem the simplest answer to why they keep retelling, adorning and getting carried away with anecdotes from their past. Then again, perhaps that endless repetition and embellishment of stories from their youth conceals the need to maintain a balance between what we once were and what we are today, for each of us installs a filter in the river of life in order to decide what to take out and what not. Some small part of us is always dying at every moment, but we seem to believe we're immortal, even at funerals of our nearest and dearest, and we construct our own personal history as if we were Caesar or Galilei. Doesn't it seem pointless to make the effort to be remembered when we know we will have to go away one day? But isn't it so very human, that flimsy significance that gives us a sense of self-satisfaction and security and tells us that we are a marvellous and unique work of the Creator just when we are at our most insignificant? Aging mitigates our megalomania of course, although I can vouch that some of my age-mates still like to think they are little heroes. Heroes with walking sticks, huh! Except for him, the eternal child, who can fly – up, up and away – and will stay as intelligent and feckless as he is forever.

And what can I say, having two such different lives behind me? I sit on a bench in Kensington Gardens, close to the autumn of life, and around me pigeons peck at the crumbs of bread I bring for them every week. Everyone has their own destiny. For example, there are some trees whose leaves begin to turn yellow and fall as early as August, like those people who experience the culmination of their life-force and attractiveness in their youth and afterwards let the years trample them down almost without resistance. As wise Horace aptly said: *Est modus in rebus, sunt certi denique fines.* Things have a proper measure, there are also definite bounds. Other trees keep their leaves until late autumn, holding on like the last proud hairs of those lonely veterans who walk the main paths of the park, elegantly dressed but each with some salient feature like a white silk handkerchief in the upper pocket of his redingote to emphasize his flight from the boring routine of family life. Ancient and too proud to go to a smoky pub, they strut through the park with their carefully maintained exteriors, as upright as possible. Even when a sudden shower of rain comes that can make a man as sopping wet in one minute as if he'd fallen in the Thames, these haughty characters open their umbrellas with all the calm in the world, as if they were opening a parasol on a summer afternoon. Some of those trees seem to have deliberately detached themselves and become like those eccentrics so typical of our Isles, and, standing alone in a meadow, they spite the wind and rain, peculiar to the very end, when they will be chopped down and their trunks mutilated to be carted away to an elegant furniture workshop or a humble, firewood market. There is another type of deciduous tree in the park, too, those which shed their golden leaves not gradually but all at once, spreading that soft aureole all around, which children and their mothers find so enchanting as they run around the tree and shower each other with the leaves. Which people correspond to those trees? *Ipso facto,* by that very fact, they have something that radiates from them, without pretence, refinement and disguise, something others perceive as a power influencing them when they are nearby or hear them speak. *Quod natura dat, nemo tollere potest.* What nature gives, no one can take away. And Peter? What kind of tree is he? Certainly not deciduous! He is self-satisfied and eternal, without signs of weakness or wear. A conifer! Yes, and in particular one of those that the skilful Japanese stop in its growth and leave small, handsome, and unchanged – a conifer bonsai!

I know that the restrictions of the social environment can sometimes stifle or, rather, subdue one's individuality. On the other hand, doesn't every mature person retain their individuality and uniqueness? Peter has personality, I agree, even if he never grows up, but I have it too. He perhaps sees more than just what is visible, and as well as that he can fly. He doesn't grow old, and it's no secret that the eyesight of children without glasses is better than that of a sixty-year-old gentleman. I have reconciled my nature with society's norms and rational expectations, but him? His only 'obligation' is to go into raptures, to fly and to swordfight with a captain lost and without a compass. He just flits about to his heart's content, coming and going as he wishes, seducing generations of poor girls and pretending to give them a new life, and all of them believe they're genuine princesses. His life is never-ending, and he amasses pleasant memories from all his past tomfoolery. Let's be honest: that makes him especially dastardly and heartless, but whoever enlightens the girls will be anathema to them for the rest of his life!

As usual, the park is full of children, governesses and dogs, but none of them dare to annoy the pigeons because they've already got to know my ill temper. They observe me and the birds from a safe distance, the children openly, the dogs furtively, but all of them are a bit scared of me as if I was old Solomon Caw, the raven whom Peter met in this very park when he flew for the first time and swore never to grow up. That aged raven, whose wise-sounding name they say is no coincidence, pitied Peter as a 'Betwixt-and-Between' (not a bird, and not a proper child either) and helped him as best he could to accept his destiny. That was not at all hard for a fellow like Peter. When we, the Lost Boys, found ourselves in Neverland, Peter was already behaving like an absolutist whose every whim is justified by divine right.

Neverland! All in all, it was an endless race: we were being chased by the pirates, they by the redskins, who in turn had constant trouble with hungry wild animals, in whose skins we were dressed. A typical uroboros, although the island wasn't exactly circular in form, but long and irregular, with bays and points; everyone was chasing everyone else or lurking in order to surprise others, or was in danger, or all that at once. But who can square the circle when it is irregular? No one can. So it was a race, running on the spot, and the soles of your feet are hot from the cry of blood, but you mustn't let weariness overcome you because your bloodthirsty pursuer just needs a few seconds to catch you! In the bedtime stories that mothers tell their children – my wife did the same with ours – there is no end to the lovely make-believe things of Neverland, although the Lost Boys and I lived on the island for years and know very well how dangerous it was. But, as the saying goes, *Quot capita tot sensus*. As many heads so many opinions.

Peter differed the most from the six of us, and I think that's maybe why he was made our leader. As I said, we had heavy, ungainly bearskin clothes, while he wore an elegant suit of leaves. He was always impulsive, both in mirth and in his snubs: 'Fly, Curly! Come on, now it's your turn, Twins! Tootles, what are you waiting for?' he ordered and roared with laughter. We clung to the ground like balls of fur, and when we tried to fly and ended up rolling on the ground we couldn't help but laugh at our own clumsiness. But, like I say, Peter was different, both in looks and in the charm and confidence with which he ruled our band. He also forbad us from trying to be like him. He always held our hand, as Michael Darling said. Although Michael was the youngest and most naïve of us all, and is thus the best placed to forget all about the world outside, now, when so many years and decades have passed (his eldest son Robert is just finishing at Eton), he revisits the images he accepted with all the exhilaration of a child during our time in Neverland. I know some complain that Michael is a chatterbox, a blabber who says things that are best left unsaid, but I enjoy his company, not just because we're related. He's a fellow who quickly relieves you of inertness with his constant yarns and jokes. His mind always wants to move along the fringes, and that makes him a bit like Peter, although he's far from having Peter's self-satisfied egotism. Both of them, I think, have a certain mannerism, an awareness of how to appeal to others, except that with Peter it's connected with Neroesque conceitedness, while Michael may be garrulous but is essentially a decent boy, never vulgar. What horrifies me most is aggressive primitivism (which has been tamed in the Empire thanks to our truth-loving Queen – long may she reign over us!), which certainly did exist in Neverland, and to be honest it was because of Peter.

Time passed quickly in Neverland and there were so many changes, both easy and painfully difficult ones, but our age didn't change. We were immortal, in a way, in our forgetting to grow, although we didn't think about it at all. Afterwards, when we were taken in by the Darling family, everything began to unfold in an orderly way, from the morning wash to Wendy's bedtime stories, in other words calmly and in moderation, without the late Captain Hook and his equally-dead pirates, may God forgive their evil souls. And without Peter, who returned to Neverland as expected. I missed him at first, I must admit. But as time went on, and after my thirteenth birthday, which we celebrated with an unforgettable party with the Darlings and my new school friends at home, in No. 14, fuzz began to grow on my chin and body, which they say is a sign of puberty and a boy's transition to adulthood. I remember that Wendy, to the approval and cheers of everyone present, agreed to cut my birthday cake, and when she leaned over the table, her short skirt rode up high, above the top of her stockings, and I caught a glimpse of her white thighs and felt (for the first time among others, which I found most embarrassing) a very male bulge in my trousers. I was almost angry at myself for a moment, but then I promised myself I would never let go of Wendy – how's that for an admission! – a promise I kept by ultimately marrying her. *Ex parvis saepe magnarum momenta rerum pendent.* Events of great consequence often spring from trifling circumstances.

Last week we went to the funeral of Barney, the youngest of 'The Twins'. He died pointlessly, on a Sunday-morning stroll in Trafalgar Square. His hearing wasn't the best, the poor fellow, and as he was crossing the street it seems he didn't hear the warning shouts of the carriage driver. The driver, who visibly felt very bad about it, said he had yelled at the top of his voice but that it hadn't been enough to alarm the man who stepped out onto the street, smiling to himself and looking into the sky. We had never spoken with Barney about serious topics like Disraeli's policies or the art of the Pre-Raphaelites; he retained his simple-hearted likeability from the time of Neverland. Everyone felt very sorry, and for Wendy it was just too much and she burst into tears.

Beneath the vigilant eye of the Darlings, all of us Lost Boys received a sound education and sufficient preliminary, material security to spare us the dissipation and wantonness of the middle classes. We needed a good profession. But all our assumptions about life were so inadequate and ultimately debutantish! Take me, on the one hand – although I'm getting on, I'm in good shape for my years, knock on wood. But I'm too old to be called up to fight in one of those senseless wars, thank God; my three sons are still hostages to that obligation, and I don't know if I should be more worried or proud of the fact. And then take Barney, who was quite the opposite. He remained a bachelor and never had the ambition to prove himself in society; a pale, guileless fellow, whom Michael often made jokes about, as well as inoffensive remarks like: 'Oh Barney, you're as soft as cotton, but cotton is so insubstantial,' and Barney would laugh about himself.

I know that Wendy, who is the same age as me, and dignified and respected as befits a lady of her status in our society, is still in love with Peter Pan. I intentionally don't say 'Peter', but 'Peter Pan', because her feelings for him and her image of him are thousands of miles and thousands of hours away from here. They're back in Neverland when she was a nine-year-old girl. And I ask myself what a mature lady, who already has a granddaughter, can recall of a time when she was so young (and in any case still asexual)? How can she still be sustaining her fantasy because of one feckless holiday heartbreaker? What did she find during her short, admittedly exciting stay in Neverland to keep her infatuated to this very day? I know that if she makes me the basis of comparison it will be to my disadvantage: Because I have a fat, unathletic body, which since the age of thirty has looked shapeless, as if under water: And because I'm predictable in my choice of what I do and say. I'm sure Wendy thinks I lack a third dimension, that my character is as flat as a playing card, as opposed to the 'lucid' mind of Peter Pan, who is able to hover in the in-betweens but still arrive on the scene and playfully take risks. I on the other hand always, at regular intervals, feel my wrists to check if the ends of my shirtsleeves are in line with those of my coat and do what's expected of me by speaking accurately, with good accent and grammar, although Michael told me with the best of intent: 'You've still got a slight twang there, dear boy, which shows you're not from a blue-blooded family'. *Habet suum venenum blanda oratio*, as they say. Sweet speech has its own venom.

In the end though, although I don't believe Wendy would make such an accusation, I must defend myself against the idea that I haven't shown enough love for our children. That's untenable and far from the truth. Perhaps I've created a certain Aristotelian distance between the different parts of the house and their functions. I never felt quite comfortable entering the children's rooms full of milky, infant smells when they were little (unlike Peter, who goes barging into children's rooms without warning, through an open window). After all, that's the business of the wet nurse and the mother. Conversely, I don't like it when Wendy or Jane come rushing into my study without knocking. It has nothing to do with love or lack thereof, but with respect for people's peace and quiet. Just as I like the sound of the newspaper I open in the mornings. I also have to admit that I tend to feel rather awkward in female company. Starting in Neverland, and all through my time at Number 14 and the years at college, I've always been mainly in a male world. From an early age, I would often have dinner at the Club, men only of course, and for years I've maintained absolutely correct friendships there in the smoking room or around the billiard table. I simply find it easier with the male of the species.

Still, despite all my dull obsessions, I'm no Mr Average. I like to wear a yellow rosebud in the lapel of my blazer, and it's my trademark at the Club. Just like I prefer medium-size cigars and find women in white fur coats particularly attractive. Isn't that quirky? Apart from that, I have a truly astounding ability to pick up and whistle the melody of the latest operetta. At the Club, that's considered characterful.

As an adopted child, like all of the Lost Boys, I took on the surname Darling. Michael used to joke that our coming to No. 14 'more than doubled the number of Darlings in just one day'. And he was right, the five original Darlings were joined by the six of us. It was a big family, to be sure, but Mr Darling was able to hold all of us in his kind arms. He gave us a good education and brought us up to be dignified subjects of the Empire. My family say I was the most likeable little blighter of the Lost Boys in Neverland – Tootles with just three teeth. But it was me whom Tinker Bell persuaded to fire the arrow at Wendy. She was flying in the air like a huge white bird and one of us, I think it was Slightly, who always pretended to remember things from before Neverland, said that 'Wendy' was the name of a bird. And as if she had been waiting exactly for that, Tinker Bell began to squeal: 'Peter wants you to shoot the Wendy. Quick Tootles, quick! Peter will be very pleased.' I obeyed her and, being an excellent shot, I hit Wendy right in the chest. I was very proud of myself when she fell to the ground, but we saw straight away that it wasn't a bird but something entirely different. Horace was spot on, *Nec semper feriet quodcumuque minabitur arcus.* An arrow does not always hit what it is aimed at. Some said it was a girl. I went pale and began to shake; I had never seen a girl before, apart from the Pretty Mama of my dreams. I remember thinking, 'Just when a real Mama comes along, I go and shoot her down.' In fact, I so felt so sorry for the evil I had done, although I had been cajoled into it by the jealous Tinker Bell, that I immediately accepted that I be punished and killed by Peter with the same arrow I had hit Wendy with. Luckily, just as I knelt and awaited my punishment, Wendy moved her hand. Someone even heard her whisper, 'Poor little Tootles...: (Although I never understood how she could have known my name). The arrow had struck her brooch, a present from Peter (a fact he often emphasized), and that saved her life.

Wendy really was a mother to us, less of her own accord than because we wanted her to be – in Neverland we needed someone to mother us and tell us bedtime stories. After we moved to London, Mrs Darling took over the role of mother, which was much more appropriate, but Wendy's protectiveness and attentiveness towards me continued, first in a sisterly sort of way, afterwards in our marriage, and I still enjoy it today in those little everyday gestures of consideration – which shoes go with a particular suit, whether I should choose a cap or a top hat when we go visiting, stopping me from drinking too much wine (a smile is enough, and she would never say anything like that out loud in company) and the like. As things turned out, I took the 'bird' I bagged, my 'mother' and my 'sister' to be my wife. As such, naturally, her surname was the same as mine: Wendy Moira Angela Darling. Or rather, mine was the same as hers. Maybe that's why our marriage has always looked respectable, as a marriage should. We also had three sons – upstanding citizens pleasing to our Queen. And also a daughter, little Jane, whom the Lord has gifted with a daughter, Margaret, my granddaughter. *Uxor bona optima possessio.* A good woman is the best possession.

Therefore I can't explain where my current insomnia comes from. In Neverland I literally slept underground, in a kind of cellar, on the hard, cold ground on an improvised bed of leaves, warmed only by the animal fur I was dressed in. Pirates may have been prowling in the menacing darkness around me, or wild animals, ghosts and creatures of the night, but I slept soundly and almost peacefully like a baby. Today, by contrast, I live in a large house, almost a palace, with maidservants and the most comfortable bedroom with a soft, king-sized mattress; yet I wake up at night restless and covered in sweat, and it's a long wait before I can go back to sleep. It's as if a pea has got under the mattress and made a lump that bores into me without end. 'That's time gnawing away at you, old boy –,' Michael said, 'we've grown old and are alone now.' 'Alone?' I queried. 'Each alone with his own aging.' And while I'm tossing and turning in bed (gummy like I was in Neverland, but sixty years older), I'm sure that no-gooder will fly into the room of my granddaughter Margaret one night, just like he flew into the room of my daughter Jane and the room of my wife Wendy. He'll sit on her bed and crow. Margaret will wake up and see a hand-some boy, but she won't realize that, beneath his fine exterior, the boy inside is particularly bad. Not because he never brushes his shoes but because he only ever cares for his own amusement. My granddaughter Margaret, like Jane and Wendy before her, will see nothing but the handsome boy who will teach her to fly and take off with her for the wonderful realm of Neverland. And it will go on like that forever, when I've long since turned to bones and then to dust; Peter Pan will keep calling on the girls and crow and whisk them away, and he will be just as immature as ever, just as young. Some geriatrics may become infantile, but he will never grow old.

When I die (of a heart attack, I imagine), my Wendy, as an esteemed widow, will be better provided for than she expects. My sons will remember me with a reverence strangely similar to the awe they used to feel in my presence. My obituary in *The Times* will be one of the most prominent in that section. I suppose Wendy, Jane and Michael will shed a tear or two at the funeral, but when they're leaving the cemetery my son will probably tell them some of his jokes to cheer them up. It will probably be all the same to me, although I assume that in the moment of death I will be filled with shock. As far as Peter is concerned, if someone happens to mention that I've died, I'm sure he'll scratch his head of unruly hair and ask: 'Tootles? Who was that again?'

Now the pigeons have also gone. They had a nice feed and cooed me a friendly farewell: 'Goodbye, till next week at the same time.' As he said – *he* being the wise Horace, of course: *Singula de nobis anni praedantur euntes.* The years as they pass plunder us of one thing after another.

'Would you ever like to go back to Neverland?' Michael asked me a few evenings ago.

'The way we are now? Certainly not.'

'You're right. It's not something I'd want either,' he laughed with the small dose of irony his cheerful nature permitted. But I knew just then that we both felt sad.

This fairy tale should not be told to a barber

Leftpatria and Rightpatria

Once, not long ago, there were two neighbouring countries –Leftpartia and Rightpartia. Leftpartia was ruled by Emperor Amos IV and Rightpartia by Samo VI. The favourite colours of the Leftpartians were violet, because it reminded them of the sweet-smelling flowers, and black because it was serious, but they didn't like white because it soiled so easily. The Rightpartians liked pink, because it reminded them of ballerinas, and white because it was the cleanest, but they were all against black because it was morbid and made people sad.

It's not hard to imagine that relations between the two neighbouring states were unstable and tended towards frosty. When they became particularly icy, it was mandatory for diplomats from Leftpartia to wear black suits, and those from Rightpartia to wear white (but warm) suits.

As is normal in such geopolitical situations, individuals sometimes emigrated from the left country to the right, or vice versa, and accordingly they started parting their hair on the opposite side quite voluntarily and changed the colour of their clothes in line with their new environment. Those who by whim of Mother Nature went bald always had wigs available to them, of different colours and lengths and with the parting on the correct side.

In addition to these fickle turncoats, there was a group of individuals who attracted criticism from both sides and were branded 'waverers', 'troublemakers', 'eggheads' or 'dreamers'. 'Fantasy is not about imagining what things could be, but about making them happen', they said in their defence, in the spirit of Karel Čapek, making it clear that they had the best of intentions; but even then they were quickly silenced by the cohorts of dynamic activists of the left and right. They tried, without discernible success, to apply the time-tested formulae of Confucius, Buddha, Horace and many others concerning moderation, the need for differentiation, respect for the values of the individual, and the middle way; but people didn't have the patience to listen to them. What?! Amos IV and Samo VI were one-hundred-percent convinced that they were the centre of the universe, and now they were supposed to enter into a dialogue with some lightweight who wasn't even a party member? Out of the question. Both sides demanded that people come down squarely 'for' or 'against', with a 'yes' or 'no'. Besides, these motley waverers particularly got on their nerves because they had no order at all in their clothing. Just imagine, they wore both white (be it milk-white, cream or light beige) and black (be it pitch, charcoal, smoke or bluish-black), and very often they combined them! And in the summertime they wore purple T-shirts with pink patterns or stripes. And what's more, with shorts!

There's no particular moral to this story because the most important agent, the electorate, is still too much tied up in the logic of black and white, us and them, at least in our region today. But the story is good enough to be linked up to another little observation to do with fantasy. Let us call it: The Owl and Blue.

"The owl is the only bird that can see the colour blue," I once read in a *Curiosities* column. As with other weird and wonderful 'facts', this one could and should be checked for accuracy, a test performed by 29% of readers, the same column says. But I belong to the other 71% who accept the idiosyncratic creations of Mother Nature *as a dreamer*.

May this be an example: the owl, as we all know, is a nocturnal bird – one of the few birds that uses its eyes much more at night than during the day. And what is there that's blue that it can see in the darkness of the forest, where greens and browns dominate? Probably just a few wild violets scattered throughout a clearing, some moss with a blueish hue, little blue berries on some bushes, and, if it comes across a river, the colour of flowing water. That's not much, you'll say, but those are still advantages other birds don't have. Not to mention the greatest and unquestionable privilege: THE SKY! The owl is able to look into the sky from the blue of early evening to the violet of sunset, and then all the way to the inky blue of midnight mentioned above, which the colour-blind call black and is as deep as an ocean of the night.

At the same time, the other birds, for whom everything is black and white, believe there is no hope for the poor owl and that it is fated to live its life in deepest darkness.

This fairy tale is to be told to artists in their youth

Papradishki

It all began with a rather unusual encounter in a first-class compartment of the Belgrade-Skopje express train. An hour and a half or two hours south of Niš, when the end of the journey was drawing near and the train began to change speed sporadically due to the rickety track – faster for one stretch, then slower for another – a young lad appeared opposite me in the empty compartment like a bolt from the blue. Out of nowhere!

I travelled to Skopje in Macedonia fairly often, almost once every two months, because I was part of a team of Belgian builders and engineers doing surveying work there. The aim of this international project was to determine whether the main city square in Skopje could withstand all the new buildings going up on it. There was concern that it would collapse, and then the River Vardar would burst its banks, or the excavations would disturb the watercourse, and then the river would first flood them and then the whole square. For those frequent visits to Macedonia I took the train, or rather several long-distance trains: from Brussels to Paris, Paris to Belgrade and Belgrade to Skopje. There was one simple reason for me choosing the railways – I'm afraid of flying. Although an aeroplane is a highly complex and effective machine, it's as if all my fear of unpredictability and chaos has become centred on flying. As a boy, I was afraid of lifts, and today that same sense of alarm and discomfort comes out as agoraphobia at the thought of an aeroplane. I'm afraid of being trapped in the plane up in that expanse of sky and dying without being able to do anything about it. I know as well as everyone else what the statistics say: that it happens very rarely, and that car crashes and even train accidents are a much more common cause of fatality. But I also know that if it does happen – you're a goner. Aeroplanes are so fast even when they're taking off, and they fly so high up. Who can help you if something goes wrong up there?

And so, despite all the stops and waits, I became used to travelling by train. I felt secure and comfortable, and I enjoyed the leisure of leaning back, nibbling at a sandwich, and reading an interesting book. I was a particularly avid consumer of detective stories. That day, too, I was engrossed in reading a murder mystery about Inspector Maigret. I must have been quite carried away because that scraggy, big-nosed and above all terrified boy turned up in the compartment without me noticing when and how. His sweat-beaded face was contorted with fear, or rather terror. He gaped around like a little animal caught in a trap, and each time he glanced towards the window, where trees and village houses flitted past beside the track, his mouth let out vowels of distress resembling a distended shriek. His hands tightly gripped a small bag tied with string, while his legs were braced against the base of the seat opposite, as if he was trying to slow down the train. Between yells, the lad repeated an incomprehensible word ending in '-shte'.

'Calme-toi, gamin. Tout va bien,' I tried to calm him.

'...ishte... adishte...,' he stammered.

'Il n'y a pas de raison d'avoir peur.'

'...radishte... pradishte...'

'Qui es-tu? D'où viens-tu?'

The unhappy lad, all a-tremble, stared now at me, now out the window of the carriage. It was clear he didn't understand my French and that I had to call for help.

But when I returned as fast as I could with the conductor, the compartment was empty and the window was wide open. I thought the poor lad must have jumped out because he had been so agitated, and I mentioned that suspicion to the conductor. We both looked out the window, and of course all we saw were the stones and trees beside the track, and green fields with blue mountains in the distance. Even if he had jumped, we would long have left that spot behind us.

The conductor, who was clearly less alarmed than me, said the boy had probably run off to another carriage and suggested I check if any of my things were missing. I considered that rather unfriendly because the lad had had a completely honest look about him, even if he had been so confused. Still, I decided to take a glance in my travel bag, and just when I opened it the regular rattle of the train was interrupted by a screech of the brakes at a bend. The conductor and I both lost our balance for a second, and some of my clothes and my toilet bag fell out onto the seats and then onto the floor together with something else. It looked like cobalt blue powder and had spilt from that little old leather bag, which the lad had clenched tighter than tight and had left behind in the compartment in his panic. I tried to brush the powder into a little heap with a moist paper towel, but every movement of my hand just spread it further over the floor in a lighter blue stain. I felt clumsy and realized it was some kind of pigment that was increasingly dying the floor the more it came into contact with water.

Oh, as usual, when I start doing something superfluous, I groaned. The conductor had departed the compartment with an undisguised sneer, leaving me to pick up my things, so fortunately he didn't see my mishap with the pigment. Then, as I was bending down and making a mess of the floor, I saw that something else had also fallen and ended up under my toilet bag. The stiff yellowish bristles of a fine paintbrush peered out from beneath it. I picked it up – it was evidently well used. The pigment powder and the brush suggested that the poor lad was in some way connected to the trade of painter – but how?

This awoke the detective spirit of Hercule Poirot in me because, as I've mentioned, I'm not just a lover of detective novels, but a Belgian myself, and after women's tennis players and comics we are best known for Poirot and Inspector Maigret. The former is a Belgian made up by a typical British lady and the latter a stocky Parisian invented by a typical Belgian. So I couldn't let the opportunity pass to delve a bit into the mystery of the strange lad in the compartment. The name 'Papradishte', which he had repeated several times, remained in my head and was hard for me to pronounce with the right accent, and later, when I arrived in Skopje and began to inquire where the place was, my Macedonian colleagues laughed at my pronunciation. They told me it was a village seven kilometres from Bogomila, another strange name reminiscent of the ancestors of the Cathars, the Bogomils – a dualist sect that originated in this part of the world. I was surprised that most of my Skopje colleagues were unaware of this interesting historical connection. And then an unexpected turn of events opened up a new page in my investigation. In the Turkish tea shop Galeria in Skopje's old bazaar, where I dropped in one January evening to warm up with a hot drink, I met a recently graduated painter from the Academy of Art (I imagine the tea shop was a meeting-place for artists, judging by its name and the collaged murals adorning its walls). In the course of our chat, I noticed that people there liked to talk about all sorts of things, and Iko, the young painter, enthusiastically shared my interest in Papradishte. He told me in English better than mine that the first noteworthy Macedonian painter, Dimitar Andonov, had been from that very village and had added the corresponding adjective, 'Papradishki', to his surname. That was the name he later became known by. In his youth, Papradishki had helped his father and his group of *zografs*... I asked him what a *zograf* was, and he explained that it had been the name for icon and fresco painters since the Byzantine Middle Ages. Iko, who with his red beard had begun to look to me like one of those young icon painters, was evidently both knowledgeable and passionate about the matter, so I couldn't restrain myself from recounting my incredible experience on the train. Iko was greatly intrigued by the story and suggested straight away that we finish our tea and that he take me to see the large, retrospective exhibition of Papradishki's work, in honour of the 150th anniversary of his birth, which was being held in the nearby former Turkish bathhouse, now a national gallery. This was too much of a coincidence to be accidental. 'As if there was some higher purpose,' the young painter said with a smile, and I felt a heightened excitement reminiscent of the thrill that seized me when I used to explore the cellars of deserted buildings on the outskirts of Brussels as a boy.

From the tea-shop, we walked along cobbled streets through puddles of dirty slush to the old stone building, which time seemed to have forgotten. The Papradishki exhibition was in the two large, rear rooms of the former bathhouse. His works were very numerous, in different formats, with many portraits and landscape paintings. And in the central space his painting utensils were exhibited: an easel with his self-portrait in profile as a ninety year-old, a low table with his paintbrushes, pigments messily packaged in paper, linseed oil, and an old wooden stool with a very worn, flattened cushion on it. Iko told me that Papradishki died painting.

'But... this is the same paintbrush and the same blue pigment as in my compartment!' my voice echoed through the acoustic space of the bathhouse.

Almost simultaneously, Iko and I realized that the next step had to be to visit Papradishki's native village.

Iko offered to drive me there, but I proposed we go by train, which would be more interesting and more in tune with our mystery. And, sure enough, we found out there was a local freight train via Veles and Bogomila to Papradishte.

The train chugged along the uphill track, creaking and puffing, and the journey of less than a hundred kilometres took almost three hours, which even for me as a railway enthusiast was a bit too slow, but the carriage, which rocked sluggishly, crowded with all sorts of passengers and the occasional startled chicken in its owner's sack, was not at all boring for me and Iko as we talked energetically or stood in silence at the windows in the corridor, looking up at the snow-covered mountains that passed us by. We got off the train in Papradishte together with several hillwalkers, whose Sunday excursion would take them to the top of the nearby mountain, whose name, as far as I remember, begins with 'Ch'. But Iko and I headed straight for the church, which rises up on a small hill in the centre of the village.

We were welcomed in the Saints Peter and Paul Church by the young, already portly priest, Methodius, who had a similar red beard to Iko, just slightly longer. We asked him if he had known Papradishki.

'Dimitar Andonov? Oh yes, I knew him. He lived to a ripe old age – he was ninety-five when he died. Although the Communists in Skopje gave him a pretty pension, he kept coming back to Papradishte.'

Then we asked Methodius if he knew anything about the artist's journeys.

'There was a particularly strange story he once told, and I thought at the time: *God forgive me for thinking he's making it up – it must be his age.* I remember the story well, although it seemed he was telling us one of his dreams. It was about one of his trips to Serbia as a young lad, at the age of fourteen. He went to see his father, Andon, who was painting frescoes in the church of St Nikola in Gnjilane. He wanted to help out and start learning the icon painter's trade. After a long and probably tiring journey on his donkey, he had made it almost to Niš, when the animal stumbled and threw the sleeping lad. The next thing he remembered he was in a train, but since trains didn't yet exist for him at that time, he got very frightened and thought it a giant, iron snake. He cowered in fear. The monster moved with astounding speed and belched clouds of smoke. The lad had ended up in some kind of narrow chamber in the bowels of the monster, and there he was met by a strangely dressed foreigner, without cap or suit but in an unusual worn out shirt and mottled blue pants, who asked him something with a strong voice, in an incomprehensible language. Then the strange man dashed out of that chamber, and poor young Dimitar got even more alarmed, thinking the man would throw him out the window when he came back. He clasped his hands and prayed to the Lord to preserve him from the monster with red-hot jaws and its minions, to deliver him from torment and dismemberment. And as he was begging and pleading like this, Dimitar said, he was blinded by a mighty flash and suddenly found himself in a ditch by the road, all scratched, terrified and shaking, near his poor donkey. Only then did he settle down enough to cry, and as he hugged the donkey and his tears rolled down its neck he realized he had left the bag with the paintbrush and pigment inside the monster.'

Partly after persuasion by Father Methodius, but more due to our reluctance to leave Papradishte straight away, we decided to spend the night in the village, with a host that Methodius recommended.

Sitting in the courtyard of the house beneath the cold, starry sky that evening, wrapped up in coats and scarves, we fortified ourselves with a tumbler of traditional Rakia and a snack of sheep's cheese brought out onto a low, wooden table by our host. I thought aloud and tried to connect my peculiar experience on the train with Methodius's story.

'The message in all this, Iko, is that things happen in this country that are out of step with time, and it would seem that even time travel is possible.'

After a brief pause, he looked at me with an intense stare and said: 'Yes, some things occur contrary to the flow of time... I can think of another example of something that happened near here, in the city of Veles. In 1855, a certain Haji Koste Krstev painted the frescoes there in the church of St Dimitria (I asked Iko to write the name in Latin letters in my notebook, which is why I can refer to him now). He signed his name beneath the frescoes and added that he was an icon painter – and photographer!'

'Sorry, but I don't see what's so strange about Mr Haji... (here I consulted my notebook again) ...Krstev adding that to his name.'

'What's strange is the year: 1855. Four years before the birth of our Papradishki, who, as I mentioned, was the last Macedonian icon-painter and first European-style painter. That means photography was accepted here much earlier than profane painting. My family album, for example, contains photographs of my great-grandfather Prokopi, taken long before Papradishki painted his canvases.'

Yes, it's hard to explain some things with logic here, even for a faithful compatriot of Hercule Poirot, I mused. The task for which I was called to Macedonia – to raise up the main square, which was sagging beneath the weight of the new buildings – is also rationally inexplicable, yet the main square still needs to be lifted. That's why I'm here as an expert, for which I'm paid a fee plus handsome per diems. Staying in the guest house, 'Lucia' by Lake Ohrid for two days hardly costs half a per diem. Not to mention the afternoons in Skopje's old bazaar with its tasty, long rissoles, kebabs, spicy bean stew and Noah's Pudding, and all for such a modest price, but with inestimable satisfaction for the palate.

'What's even more interesting,' Iko continued, 'is that Papradishki painted a great number of self-portraits at different periods of his life. Or, to be precise, he painted himself as a fifteen-year-old boy when he was already in his mature years. And it's crystal clear that the fifteen-year-old on the canvas is not a reflection from the mirror, but the reflection of another time in his life, a much earlier one, preserved on one of his photographs. He used his old photographs to paint self-portraits.'

We each drank another tumbler or two of Rakia to warm ourselves before going to bed in the unheated room, but it was warm enough under the homemade blankets on the two cast-iron beds. I huddled, exhausted, under the shaggy, woollen covers and was soon fast asleep. I dreamed a muddle of queer things, but in the morning my last dream was clear in my head.

I dreamed I was in front of the open front door of a house as square as a box. I was being shown out by a short, plump man with a trimmed moustache, neatly dressed. I noticed that his shoes were freshly polished. He was wearing a light-grey hat.

'Quel beau paysage,' the man said, although you wouldn't have thought, to judge by the expression on his well-groomed, friendly face, that he was necessarily a nature lover: 'Off you go, my friend, it's time – the train won't wait for you. Your place is among the living. I'll stay behind with the dead,' and finally he added in a voice that was clear and resonant even in the dream: 'A bientôt, mon ami.'

I wanted to tell him that he would remain with me, but in the dream I was now already travelling in a train. It was much more modern and faster than the one I had come to Papradishte on; it seemed not to be travelling on rails (there was none of the usual click-clacking) but to be gliding along. I was in a compartment with a younger man in jeans and a faded T-shirt which once, a long time ago, had been the favourite clothes of the young generation. The young man stared at me in dismay.

I felt the train accelerate.

This fairy tale should not be told
while eating frogs' legs for dinner

The Haji, the Shoemaker
and the Fool

A haji, a shoemaker and a fool started out on a long journey together.

Each was travelling for his own reasons. The haji in order to reach 'The Goal' and crown his years of spiritual effort. The shoemaker because he knew the haji's shoes, and those of other hajis, would wear out on the long journey, and that then they would need somebody to mend them or offer them new ones; at an affordable price, of course; and the fool because he had found company.

They walked on like that for one day, and another, and the fool became tired. So he suggested to the haji that he could ride on his back for a few miles until he had got his breath back. The haji took this as a sign from the Almighty – a test of his faith – so he accepted. He carried the fool not just for a few miles, and not for a dozen, but for twenty miles and more, all the time weighed down by the fool, but with virtuous thoughts, until his shoes were completely worn out and the soles were falling apart. Then the shoemaker suggested a pair of virtually new ones, at an affordable price. The haji bought them with gratitude and paid him double.

They continued on their way. After a time, they came to a small lake, actually more of a big puddle, with a lot of tadpoles and the odd frog. The largest frog was their queen and she also possessed magic powers. It hopped up onto a rock and stared at the travellers. The shoemaker was about to chase it away, but the haji stopped him with the words: 'It too is one of God's creatures, just like you and I.' Meanwhile, the fool waded into the puddle and spoke to it: 'Do you grant wishes?' The frog replied quite calmly, as if it had

105

been expecting the question: 'Well, yes. But since there are three of you, you shall only have one wish each.'

The shoemaker spoke first: 'Give me a manufactory' (being a greedy fellow, he actually said 'moneyfactory', but the frog knew what he meant). The haji, after brief reflection, pronounced: 'My only aim is to reach to 'The Goal'. The longer and more uncertain the journey, the greater my reward will be at the end.' But the fool just gazed with eyes as bulbous as a frog's and yelled: 'I want to be a politician!'

The shoemaker returned home to find a building with the sign 'Manufactory'. After a while of making shoes by hand, he moved into trading second-hand cars.

Many years later, the haji also returned – grey-haired, wrinkled and ill, but happy. A week or so later, he died with a smile on his face.

When the fool finally made it home, he saw an expensive, modern limousine in front of his house, with a uniformed driver at the wheel, and behind it was parked another limousine with two shaven-headed men in suits (but with no driver). And so the fool became a politician. The voters entrusted him with a second four-year term in office. In the meantime, as you know, the haji died, but the shoemaker became a friend and associate of the fool.

The fool moved into a palace on a hilltop, called *The Residence*, in the most exclusive part of the city. He lived there without a care, except that in the evenings a host of frogs would gather around the palace and croak *riddup, riddup, riddup*, all night long.

This fairy tale is to be told to postgraduates in seminars on 'Elites and Mass Culture'

Homunculus

He found his teacher standing by the glass dome and studying the homunculus with visible interest. 'Hello, come closer,' he invited his apprentice, not turning his eyes from the object of his preoccupation. 'Don't you think he's grown since last night?'

To judge by the shadows under his teacher's eyes, he had clearly spent a sleepless night, but his eyes sparkled like those of a vivacious old lover: 'Look, he's started moving.'

It seemed that the little man beneath the glass dome, or what was supposed to resemble a man, still lay motionless. His lips had already formed, as had his hands, penis and clumsy-looking feet, which seemed disproportionately large compared with the amorphous mass they had grown from. 'He's developing very quickly. Do you think he can see us?' Alcibiades whispered, as excited as a child, without waiting for Bonifacio to answer. But whatever he replied, in approval or not, his teacher would not have heard him. Ever since digging up the large mandrake root from below the gallows on Friday morning before dawn, and bringing it here to incubate beneath the dome, he had done everything necessary for the homunculus' organism to start working. The process was complex from the very beginning: the mandrake root had to be separated from the soil most attentively; thick, double-layered pigskin gloves were often used for the purpose because the mandrake could react erratically and release noxious, oily droplets while being dug up. Sometimes dogs were used to pull the root out of the ground with their teeth, and sometimes the dog died in agony. Although his teacher had already mastered the skill of cultivating and extracting mandrake, he was ever cautious and meticulous. He nourished this strange fruit with honey, milk and the blood of a freshly killed young rooster. He made a moist, nutritious bed for it from the clumps of earth beneath the hanged man, still imbued with the last drops of his sperm, and enriched it with forty-day-old horse manure. That was the established procedure, by which Alcibiades had already created several mute homunculi, whom he used as miniature servants or acrobats for entertainment. Their short lifespan – four months at most – in no way diminished their impressiveness, which a small circle of the teacher's trusted friends were able to convince themselves of when he invited them to presentations of the homunculi. In contrast to mechanical figures in the form of paradisiacal birds, bees or lutists, who chirped and buzzed or played a primitive melody on two strings (far from the skill of Francesco da Milano), only to tire after those few minutes of activity and revert to a stiff, inanimate state; homunculi, despite their ungainly, unattractive bodies and misshapen extremities (one arm or leg is usually shorter than the other), 'live' from the beginning to the end of their existence. It couldn't be said, however, that their birth and death resembled that of human beings or any other creature from the world of the living. Raised from a mandrake root, germinated with the sperm of a man who had met a violent end – here Thanatos completely assumed the role of Eros – they truly were children of death. Their departure from this world was also inhuman. When they felt their judgement day was nigh, these otherwise obedient creatures would become increasingly agitated and nervous; they fidgeted and had a constant need to move through the whole house with frustration written on their misshapen faces. Since they were unable to speak, they would let out a mournful but at the same time angry sound, something between a squeal and a snarl. And when it grew dark, they would start scratching and banging against the windows like a cat or dog that wants to go out to relieve itself. For Bonifacio, the most enigmatic and terrible thing was that the homunculi only ever left the house and vanished at night-time. During the day, even when they were clearly at the end of their strength, they remained indoors. They would creep away into a dark corner of the house and whimper for hours, waiting for the night. Alcibiades taught him that they waited for the sunset hour and then, without turning round to say farewell, went away forever into the night.

"'Where do they go? What happens to them?" you ask. 'There's something unfathomable and other-wordly here, my good Bonifacio, and I think the mystery of time has to be resolved differently with them than with us humans. But even that creature would not be able to be born without a man's seed, even if it was ejected in agony. The seed of a hanged man is made fecund in the womb of the earth. In other words, already in the act of being born this *omino* shatters the illusion that life is an episode with a clear, inexorable transition from beginning to end. Quite the opposite: being born literally from the end, with the sperm of death, the homunculus scoffs at the cruel joke imposed on us: that we believe time is always moving in one direction, and that aging is irreversible. This *omino* will demonstrate the opposite!'

Bonifacio was the most immediate and astonished witness of this obsession. His teacher would simply not be separated from the incubating creature beneath the glass dome, which he fed with chokeberries, catfish caviar and oil of St John's wort.

For Bonifacio, this was the seventh year since Alcibiades had taken him on as his apprentice. He still remembered his induction – it had been far from easy, although his uncle, one of the richest nobles in the city, had put in a good word for him. His teacher had invited him to his house, which was also his laboratory. Bonifacio was already eighteen and had just read *De hominis dignitate*, but that in no way helped him feel poised and self-confident. The examination lasted three days. The questions posed to him at the beginning were such that he was able to answer them outright and clearly, without delay: they concerned chronomatics, the basics of the magic square, how to make atramentum turn red and then dissolve in water, the dualistic nature of salmiac, and the interpretation of the calendar by days, ten-day periods and cycles of the moon. But when his teacher asked for astromathematics to be applied to specific medicinal issues, for instance the functioning of the thymus and the heart depending on the influence of the sun, the workings of the lungs in relation to Mercury, and the behaviour of the eyes and of bile in conjunction with Mars, Bonifacio would ponder and then try hard to give as concise an answer as possible; and then listened attentively to Alcibiades's subsequent explanations. But on the last day of the examination, when the questions entered secret, hidden spheres, concerning the astral spirits populating and ruling the heavenly bodies, and via them people's souls, or concerning the builder-spirits who create the energy chains, or concerning the scribe-spirits who leave testimony to how those energies are used for counsel, prophesy and curation, Bonifacio's cheeks burned as if he was a little abecedarian, both aroused and frightened, as he waited in silence to hear what his teacher would say. Alcibiades was evidently satisfied with his examinee's demeanour.

'Your knowledge is equivocal –,' he said, 'sometimes, you're sure you know and you clutter your answer with excessive words. Other times, afraid you don't know, you're sparing of words or go quiet altogether. Like in music, in the former case the melody is over-laden, while in the latter the few notes gain depth due to the pauses. As of tomorrow, the doors of my house are open to you. We will work together. The effort will be large for you at first and the satisfaction perhaps small, but in time, once you've built the foundations of your castle in the clouds, you won't be able to live anywhere else.'

Alcibiades was in fact speaking about the composition that was his own life (to borrow a metaphor from music that he often used himself), but he proved to be right: despite their differences in character, Bonifacio applied himself with dedication and unflagging interest over those seven years to 'fill his Temple with sculptures and harmony', as his teacher put it, enabling him to 'devote himself independently to the mystery of wisdom'.

In spite of his valiantly acquired knowledge of many things, Bonifacio didn't lose a single bit of his natural childish curiosity as he drew closer to his teacher during their years together. The immediacy with which Alcibiades involved him in his experiments could cover him with goose bumps or bring an uncontrollable grin to his face, depending on whether his conjectures were challenged or confirmed.

'Do you think he can see us? What kind of image of us is he forming in his eyes? Is he asking himself: Are they real? Do they exist? Do I exist?'

Standing tensely beside his teacher, who was leaning in front of the glass dome in his excitement, Bonifacio could not suppress the feeling that they were now heading in the wrong direction and were in immediate danger of colliding with something dark and ominous. He remembered what his teacher had said to him late one evening after he had prepared a few jars of an ointment under his supervision, a mixture of aniseed, onion, olive oil and basil for ear infections and pains: 'There, now you've learnt to make this medicine too. As an apprentice sailing the sea of knowledge, I hope my small help will aid you in arriving on the opposite shore. But no one else but you, my good Bonifacio, with your own effort, devotion and courage, will be able to reach the opposite shore of the sea that people call Time.'

Now, as he watched and listened as Alcibiades followed the growth of the homunculus almost in ecstasy, Bonifacio thought that he, unlike his teacher, would never be able to reach the shore called Time.

'My good Bonifacio, for me there is one single reason why it is so important to make this homunculus much more perfect than the previous ones: For the sake of the Truth. To create a body – a glove – but also a mind, which is the hand that fits perfectly into that glove. You know that when we lose our body, if we have come far enough on our earthly path, we may be able to see the astral dimension of all things; we may, for example through our dreams, even be able to influence someone's thoughts; but we will hardly be able to communicate at a physical level, body to body. But in this way, through the homunculus...'

'Do you mean through his alter ego?'

'Precisely. Because he, an innocent man who was hung, shall once again feel the pulsation and pull of physical matter.'

'But wouldn't that be a two-way process? Wouldn't the homunculus, or rather the hanged man, pulsate and pull the world off balance, and us with it?'

'That is exactly what I seek!' Alcibiades exclaimed, standing tall. His eyes burned with an almost netherworldly depth. 'Then the truth will be revealed!'

'So that's why you're putting so much effort into getting this homunculus to speak...'

'And speak he will: With his own voice – the voice of Count Mauricio Benedetti. So we will know what really happened.'

'But he was convicted of murder,' Bonifacio mumbled, unsure of himself.

'And by whose order was he hung, I ask you? Who was it that wanted Count Benedetti dead? I am a man of science, my good Bonifacio, not a politician. I am interested in power over chemical processes, not power over people. But even if I was a politician, I wouldn't rule with such heartless cruelty towards my opponents as our men at court do.'

'Our rulers?' Bonifacio blurted, only to realize straight away how hypocritical his humility was.

'Yes, our rulers... woe betide anyone who dares to speak out against them. They will reward him handsomely: he will be swallowed up by the night, without a sound, without a trace, quite painlessly,' Alcibiades said, with unconcealed contempt. 'And it serves the people right. They are scared to the marrow and therefore gullible and easy to manipulate.'

'But they built the university. And scholars were invited to the palace from Florence: Poliziano, Ficino, Mirandola...'

'I know, I was there, and I listened to them with admiration, and also with a good deal of criticism. But, my good Bonifacio, our so-called masters' undeniable affinity for lectures, solemn speeches and banquets has nothing at all to do with the pitiful servility of the citizenry, let alone their ignorance. Count Benedetti was one of the few who were so bold as to openly criticize those in power for their pomp and their neglect of ordinary mortals. You'll agree that ceremonies cannot be a replacement for real life, although they can be used to create a semblance of it. The count's trial for the murder of his brother and Alessandra di Prana was precisely such an orchestrated event – he was framed. I'm convinced it was a ruse by the authorities to get rid of their adversary.'

Alcibiades inscribed letters on the body of the homunculus with a white quill, letters in dark red, like blood, among which

Bonifacio recognized Latin, Hebrew and Greek characters, but the others were foreign to him. Before he could even ask, his teacher answered:

'Those are letters of the angular Glagolithic script, older than the rounded Cyrillic alphabet: It was brought to Rome centuries ago by Constantine the Philosopher together with the relics of Saint Clement of Rome, and the first to spread it were Anastasius the Librarian and Gaudericus of Velletri. Even today, the letters are still alive on the Adriatic island of Veglia, which the Slavs call Krk, in the Dalmatian city of Zadar, and also further north along the coast.'

Bonifacio nodded, although the swiftly spoken medley of information had not yet sunk in. He had learnt to listen to his teacher and memorize what he said, and to fill in the gaps in his knowledge later, using the glossaries in the library.

'I'm marking Glagolithic on him in addition to the Latin, Greek and Hebrew alphabets to instil in him the logos that links pure ideas to reality. I'm drawing word stems on him and feeding him with letters. The branches spread and the letters help them interlock with other word stems and complement each other. That's why I write them in different alphabets – so that the shape, order and use of the letters become etched in his mind; so that he will learn them and be able to speak. That's also why the quill I'm drawing the letters with is a swan's wing feather. For there are magic spells that can turn a swan into a human being, and vice versa, and Zeus used the guise of a swan to seduce Leda. The red colour is from beetroot juice. Thick, nine times concentrated, so it acts lastingly and reliably.'

Despite having been applied very delicately, the red letters penetrated the skin of the homunculus, but gradually. Even ten days after application the lines and shapes of the letters were still visible. But the homunculus made no sound.

'Teacher, he still hasn't spoken.'

'Be patient, Bonifacio. When the sickle moon in the mirror is like it was when I wrote the letters, the time will come for you to hear his voice.'

'Sorry for my confusion but this is all new and unexpected for me...'

'Quiet –,' Alcibiades interrupted him, 'look, he's breathing!'

The candlestick illuminating the glass dome was at the very edge of the table, and Bonifacio had to move it a little towards the middle. It magnified the scene where the homunculus lay, making him look as if he had been placed on an enormous, dark rectangle much larger than the table. The hideous, distorted baby was growing quickly. The candlelight now cast a pale sallowness on the face of the homunculus, whose waxen skin, and particularly his irregular features, made him look other-worldy: the left eye higher than the right, the bristly red tufts of hair that looked like a broom-maker's experiment, and the oversized, soft lips, all of which gave the face of the omino an unnatural bloatedness. As Bonifacio looked at that unlovely physiognomy, the air around him seemed to become dense and stifling, as if the room had not been aired for a long time.

He lowered his gaze towards the creature's naked, hairless ribcage, which rose and fell in a rapid rhythm, like when someone is running or lifting a heavy load – like a sequence of sighs in quick succession, chasing each other.

'Let's take off the top of the dome so he can breathe better,' his teacher urged, although the dome had enough small openings to allow a flow of air. Alcibiades was so impatient that he almost dropped the glass top as he was lifting it. Bonifacio wondered when he had last seen his teacher so excited.

'There, that's him. He's here...'

The breathing of the homunculus seemed to become louder, and they heard a strange, 'agrr... agrr... akrr...' from between his swollen lips, almost like a word. And again: 'Agrr... agrr... akrr...' They could even make out a hint of the diphthong 'ao' squeezing its way out amidst the heavy breathing.

'I recognize him, Bonifacio ... I know that fragments of thoughts that belonged to Count Mauricio are coalescing in his head, and I recognize his restlessness... Don't hold back – ask me what's troubling you. Do you doubt that he'll speak? Come on now, esteemed Bonifacio (was there a hint of derision in that form of address?), our reason comes from God and therefore we must believe it. Everything that exists in this world exists for a purpose. The compass, so we know where we've set off from and where we're going. Gunpowder, so we know how to kill at a distance. Pig-faced men and Amazons, not so we know who they are, but who we are.'

Filled with a shaking and bewilderment, Bonifacio followed his teacher's high-spirited declaration: 'Therefore, from tonight, he will be given a name: Mauricio (Bonifacio pronounced it together with him). We will speak to him as if he has been reborn. I am returning him to life, Bonifacio – I am reviving Count Mauricio.'

His teacher had named the previous homunculi by numbers (which, to Bonifacio's mind, sounded much too cheerful for their sad destinies): Primo, Secondo, Terzo. This homunculus was the ninth in sequence and so it should have been given the name Nono, but that would have been too ordinary; this one was to be different and special, and his teacher attached great meaning to his existence.

Most inhabitants of the Republic considered the trial and execution of Count Mauricio Benedetti a case of premeditated, judicial murder, but it was an act of courage for anyone to say that, even in a whisper, because spies lurked behind every corner, and punishment came fast and on silent feet. The notable Benedetti family had been virtually peerless in elegance and wealth for decades. The late Bernardo, father of Mauricio and his younger brother Giacopo, had served the city capably for many years as a member of The Six – the highest council of the city, which effectively ruled the Republic. It was treated as a matter of course that his son, Mauricio, would later take his place. But that did not happen, at least not immediately. Officials issued a hypocritical public statement announcing cunningly, some would say perfidiously, that a certain time was required in order to review the public conduct of Count Mauricio, who had shown through a series of incidents that he was of a violent nature and as such unsuitable for such a high and responsible public office. It was true that Mauricio lacked the inherent magnanimity of his father and that he was inclined to quarrels and brawls, but could that not be said of quite a number of young men in the city? They were ruled by the element of fire, choler, hot and dry, the fruit of impatient youth: But the fact that Count Mauricio's choleric nature was so pronounced was used against him by his powerful rivals in order to destroy him, the teacher told Bonifacio.

It was like this: Count Mauricio Benedetti had been married to the most beautiful woman in the city for three years. Bonifacio had once had the rare opportunity to see Alessandra di Prana, later Countess Benedetti, when she passed by him in the street. Like everyone else who encountered her, he was struck and dumb-founded by her exceptional attractiveness. She was five or six years older than him, which, seeing as Bonifacio was still very much a boy, can be considered a significant difference in age, but her beauty was an essence untouched by time, like that of Helen of Troy or Simonetta Vespucci, and she completely deserved the nickname by which she was known throughout the city: La Bella. She had a pronounced pale complexion, highlighted by her lush auburn hair crowned by a diadem of pearls. The women of the city spared no expense to at least approximate her delicate pallor, and it was no secret for Bonifacio that a considerable part of his teacher's earnings came precisely from the skin lightening creams ordered by such ladies. With Alessandra di Prana, this delicate complexion and the dark, flaming curls of her hair were a gift of nature or of God. What the enchanted beholder (ashamed by the openness of his admiration) discovered to be La Bella's third wonder were her almond-shaped, honey-brown eyes, which could even have been judged melancholic had they not shot forth a daring, open, even piercing gaze, which caused yet more amazement.

Even as a child, Bonifacio had heard the stories about La Bella that were told throughout the city: about her beauty, above all, but also to do with her beautiful singing and musicianship on the gamba and flute. It was also said that she wrote romantic poetry, with subtle ornamental elegance, which she kept for herself and her closest circle. Therefore the announcement of her marriage to Count Mauricio Benedetti, a boor and meat-head without style, caused general aston-ishment. There were rumours among ladies of advanced years that she had perhaps been forced into wedlock due to the wealth of the Count. Alessandra di Prana was from one of the oldest but especially impoverished families, and this was a last opportunity for her to marry into a wealthy house. But why then did her father not choose the younger Count Benedetti, Giacopo, the rumour-mongering continued, who in contrast to his elder brother was of a playful disposition, a lover of the Arts, and in any case much more suitable as a husband for the beautiful Alessandra. The answer was that Count Mauricio was the first-born and therefore possessed the Benedettis' fortune, and also that he himself had been planning for some time to make this lovely noblewoman the mother of his children. In this city proud of its broad-mindedness and its playful, piquant canzonettas and frottolas, women were required to lay aside their colourful tunics after six years of marriage and to wear black. They were allowed to keep their high, ruffled collars and wide sleeves for the time being, but after twelve years of marriage these too were banned.

'We're not doing anything sacrilegious, Bonifacio, if that's what frightens you. We're not just reviving a man but aiming to rectify the great injustice that was done to him. The Lord favours those who labour, who endeavour to fulfil their mission in life – call it duty if you like – rather than those who are motionless and passive, thinking that church every Sunday is their only duty. If we succeed in bringing back Count Mauricio, he might not have the same physical form as before, but perhaps he will speak the truth he was prevented from saying in front of his would-be judges. As Pico della Mirandola wrote so lucidly: *The Lord gave man the choice as to what form he would take on Earth. If he chooses to live like a vegetable, he will be a vegetable. If he chooses to live like a dog, he will be a dog. But if he chooses to be a man, then he also elects the way in which he exists. Like the body of a man, this body of the homunculus is also mortal and final – very short-lived in fact – but it will enable us to bring back the soul of Count Mauricio so it can tell us what I am firmly convinced of: that he is innocent.'*

The citizens of the Republic were used to dark, shadowy events, but the murder caused general horror. Who could be so monstrous as to slay beautiful, beloved Alessandra di Prana and debonair Count Giacopo?

Alcibiades was immediately summoned to the scene of the crime, since he was also highly esteemed as a master of medicine, with knowledge of Hippocrates, Galen, Aristotle and the teachers of the Salerno-Montpellier school, which he applied effectively to his patients.

'The lady was already dead,' he recalled, 'and Count Giacopo was at death's door, with his heart faltering and a pulse like a mouse's tail.' (Here Bonifacio had to ask himself again what was meant by 'mouse's tail': "When you place four fingers on the vein, you hardly feel the pulse beneath your first finger; beneath the second it is clearer, beneath the third it is clearer still, but beneath the fourth it is non-existent. Such a pulse heralds a fatal outcome.") 'It was a terrible sight – the deep gash in the upper part of the neck, right under the chin, had cut the veins and tendons, as if it had been inflicted with the precision of a professional killer. Blood still poured from the wound. The man's eyes were open wide and he was trying to say something, but it was garbled as if a rag had been stuffed into his mouth. I leaned over him and managed to discern the words: "C'e una speranza di salvezza." There is hope of salvation. Yes, my good Bonifacio, he said exactly that: There is hope of salvation. Those were his last words, and then there was just a gurgle of agony and he consigned himself to death.'

Count Mauricio was immediately arrested and accused of the double murder due to jealousy. He was quickly tried and sentenced to death by hanging. His friends pleaded that time should be allowed for judicial procedure and the gathering of counter-evidence, but it didn't help.

'There was certainly cause for doubt, my good Bonifacio. Why was Count Giacopo liquidated in such a way, not with a stab in the chest in a duel, as would have been expected from a temperament like his brother's? And why did Alessandra di Prana have to die? Mauricio Benedetti may have been a loudmouth and a bully, but he would never have killed a woman in cold blood.'

Just a few days after the murder, Count Mauricio Benedetti was walked to the gallows with wrath in his eyes and curses on his lips. *I'll be back to have my revenge, you miserable bastards!*, he shouted before he was hung.

'He departed in fury, with screams and fire.'

The homunculus no longer needed the protection of the glass dome. Soon he was up and moving, teetering like the previous homunculi, except that his first steps were harder for him because he was larger. And so, beneath the protective eye of Alcibiades, he tottered clumsily through the house with one leg longer than the other, muttering as he went, and lingering with interest in front of the iron bed, the library full of old manuscripts, and the shelves of test tubes. He even tried to grasp one of them, but it slipped through his fingers and smashed on the floor (a good thing it was empty, Bonifacio thought). His teacher immediately came running to pick up the pieces.

'Are you all right, Mauricio? You didn't get hurt, did you?' he asked with concern.

'Aka.'

'Pardon?'

'Akua.'

'Acqua! Bonifacio, he said *acqua*! He wants a drink of water. That's what I call lucid!' his teacher exclaimed and began to hop and dance like a child.

'From now on, Bonifacio, he'll sit at the table with us and we'll dine together,' he pronounced, after he had calmed down.

Bonifacio found the notion of dining rather funny because his teacher, immersed in his work, often skipped meals, and when he did eat it was mostly just a slice of bread with a clove of garlic and a glass of light wine. But now, beaming with pride, he set the dining table with an embroidered Flemish cloth and the silver cutlery reserved for special occasions. The meal began with a stew of dried vegetables, which the homunculus scoffed down with relish. 'More,' he grunted as he devoured the last mouthful. His teacher looked overjoyed, and every new nasal mutter from the homunculus as he bolted down the next course – rabbit in fermented fish sauce, and cabbage seasoned with garlic – was greeted with a storm of enthusiasm. Despite the slurred pronunciation, Bonifacio was awestruck by the precision with which the homunculus hit on words, as if he knew them from before.

At the end of the meal, his teacher poured them mead, a drink with a mellowing effect. He filled his and Bonifacio's silver goblets to the brim but only poured half a goblet for Mauricio, whom he addressed either by name, or as 'Count'. The homunculus downed the honey drink in one draught and immediately called for 'black Burgundy', which he pronounced with astonishing clarity. The dinner, marked by the homunculus's enormous appetite and his murmurings, which repeatedly brought exclamations of delight from Alcibiades, lasted late into the night, although for Bonifacio everything was somehow unreal and condensed. Finally, his teacher and the homunculus Mauricio saw Bonifacio to the door and together wished him, 'Buona notte'.

As he was walking towards his parents' house along the city's narrow alleyways, Bonifacio could not shake off the disturbing thought that, unlike the last few nights when he left for home tired after long hours of work, but calm, that night he should not have left his teacher alone. Alone with a dangerous, immoderate creature that with every movement more and more resembled the true Count Mauricio Benedetti, who could be a brutal beast in his attacks of uncontrollable rage. In Bonifacio's thoughts, the whole ritual with the homunculus and the mystery of what happens after death towered like a dark cloud above his vulnerable teacher. 'So what are you waiting for? Go straight back!' he commanded himself. He ran and ran until, panting and frightened, he arrived back at his teacher's house.

The front entrance gaped half-open, and groans came from the dining room. Among a mess of vessels, goblets and remains of food, his teacher, Alcibiades lay writhing on the floor with a stab wound in his chest like one of those with which people cut into a roast rabbit.

'That Mauricio... a mistake... not natural... the operation... a bad idea.'

Bonifacio imagined the Count leaving into the night, limping in one leg along the dark alleyways to the gates of the city, and then beyond, who knows where to – a malicious creature capable of every kind of crime.

'That project... that gripped my thinking... to bring him back... to re-examine Time... I have jettisoned it... into the night.'

'Everything will be all right, teacher. Just take it slowly. Don't strain. Everything will be alright.'

'... to give it back to God... and its old measure... unattainable for man... Time...'

As he carefully laid a silk cushion beneath the wounded man's head, Bonifacio didn't know and couldn't have imagined that, centuries later, an alchemist of verse, under the androgynous name Rainer Maria, in the shackles of synchronization invisible to the unlearned eye, would express the message his teacher seemed to be speaking in his faltering voice, with very much the same words:

A project which, at length, had gripped his thinking
That final night he jettisoned – he gave
It back to God. (Clearly the scale was wrong!)
Muttering like one who has been drinking...

This fairy tale is to be told while trying to
cut the fingernails on your right hand.

Once Upon a Prokopiev

Everything is a miracle. It's a miracle that you
don't dissolve in your bath like a lump of sugar.

PICASSO

It has been said by a variety of good writers that reality holds more surprises than dreams do. I'm convinced of it. You can dream of unicorns and other fabled creatures, you can dream of floating cubes in the middle of nowhere with ladders leading up to them, but if your life begins like Prokopiev's, you'll quickly realize that miracles are an everyday occurrence. Although, in Prokopiev's case, the miracle was actually witnessed by his mother, and he – if you'll forgive this moment of immodesty – was the miracle. But let's not prolong this introduction and get down to what happened.

When the doctor told Prokopiev's mother that she had delivered a large, healthy baby boy (weighing almost six kilogrammes), she immediately forgot all the pains of labour and looked forward to seeing her child for the first time. In that most natural state of excitement she didn't notice the bewilderment of the nurse who brought her the baby. She could hardly wait to cuddle her little boy and put him to her breast. And then – what a shock!

'That –,' Prokopiev's mother says even today with visible trepidation, 'was not a baby.' According to her description, 'it' didn't even look like a human being: it was a real little werewolf! Admittedly of the smaller variety (weighing only six kilogrammes), but covered from head to toe in thick, dark hair. And then 'that shaggy thing' began to cry. His poor mother didn't hear the crying of her baby but the howling of a wolf.

There is a rational, physiological explanation: the fruit of her womb (in other words, Prokopiev) was born with so much hair due to a hormone imbalance during pregnancy. Afterwards the hair gradually fell out, of course, but for a long time – decades, in fact – Prokopiev's mother was unable to recount that first episode of his earthly existence without feeling stressed.

After such a beginning, Prokopiev's subsequent life was inclined to proliferate strange events and experiences, and they really could serve as the basis for several interesting books. Contrary to his long-term conviction that writing literature is more than the simple rehashing of anecdotes – sometimes fragments of experience like this join together with his fantasy. The results look like weird phantasmagorias, although they are just ordinary things that happened in life.

* * *

In the springtime, when Prokopiev walked towards the south of the city, where new buildings were not yet growing faster than the trees, he would raise his eyes to the mountain: The newly built residential blocks looked like pink mushrooms growing in the shelter of its mighty green. Although he would sometimes be inspired by the 'skin and bones' of architectural creations, Prokopiev was above all a plant-lover. The houses he has lived in since his childhood have always had large gardens, and he grew up among apple trees, tomato plants, roses and the occasional whispering tree (with the birch being his clear favourite). The dancing shadows of the trees were also linked for him to the game of ping-pong.

When Prokopiev went to train with the youth team at Rabotnichki Sports Club every Tuesday and Friday afternoon, his way to the hall and back led through the City Park. This large park, one of the most beautiful in the Balkans, is home to lush stands of poplars, oaks, firs and pines. Sometimes he would stop and sit down on one of the benches, and occasionally he would read. Believe it or not, Prokopiev had a book or two in his satchel along with his bat, a number of ping-pong balls, a towel and a change of T-shirt.

He would give his all at training and, still puffed and red in the face, with his energy greatly reduced but with a clear and inquisitive head, he would devote himself to a book. There on the park bench his thoughts multiplied with the chirping of the birds. He would read until it started to get dark, which in the autumn could be a good hour later than in the winter, when the darkness crept up very fast, almost without warning, not letting him read more than two pages. Prokopiev didn't have regular training sessions in the summertime, but he had grown rather accustomed to passing the afternoons with a book in the city park. Sometimes an amorous couple would stroll past his bench, fused with each other, or a sad, solitary smoker, drawing in the acrid smoke of his cigarette and looking equally bitter to match. But after a quick glance at the passers-by, Prokopiev continued reading with passion. He would later note: *In the park in the evenings, an addle-headed lad didn't know which way to turn, not because of a girl (he hadn't even had his first kiss yet) but because of Raskolnikov, who fairly blew his mind, so that all the little pieces scintillated like mad and settled in layers of mystical feeling and ideas.* Perhaps it was precisely because of the park, that beautiful forest with its sumptuous leaves, that he fell in love with books and daydreamed, as happens when people are in love for the first time.

* * *

Still, of all the trees, as we said earlier, he most loved birches. His father, who would soon fall ill and die, but was then still well-knit, and full of charm and pride, which brought life-long friendships as well as dangerous enmities, gave him a tiny little birch for his birthday, and he planted it in the garden right under his bedroom window. That was an unusual present, and at the time Prokopiev thought his physical and intellectual development would be tied to the growth of the birch from them on. And that's how he treated it – lovingly and caringly, and a few years later, when both he and the birch had grown a little, he wrote his first poem, dedicated to it:

Slowly the tree whispers
by the walls of
my room.
It grows every year
in peace,
its stem
is like the earth,
and I remember
my small, childish hand
was once able
to close around it.
Today we're older,
and it too speaks
ever less often
about our childhood.
It has been a long time
since my hands
were able
to encircle
its closeness.

* * *

One time a girl asked him to walk her on a leash. It was one of those very thin ones, as elastic as the tip of a tongue, and he fastened it around her neck. Although he felt slightly awkward while putting it on her (she submissively bent her head so that he could attach it more easily), he felt a crest of heat in his chest as if this was something illicit, yet at the same time exciting and not to be turned down. Then he took her out for a walk on the leash like that, stopping from time to time to show her to his friends. Afterwards he led her away with a light, brisk step, almost at a run like someone coming down from Mount Vodno (and she trotted along compliantly behind him) to the garret where the boys from his circle of friends went with their 'pieces'. He was the only one who hadn't had sex yet, but that evening, although the girl looked so charitable and obedient, Prokopiev wanted to leave again as soon as they had unlocked the door of the garret. Squinting in the yellow light of the low ceiling lamp, he hung around while the girl handed him her dress. Like a frisky young animal, she also coyly but willingly rid herself of her bra and knickers, which he took with sweaty palms; his manhood limp. Then he wheeled around and left the garret with her dress and underwear, locking the naked, submissive girl inside.

That night he dreamed of a tall, mumbling old man in a purple-red tunic. It was an autumn day in the dream, but sunny, and the old man sat alone and cross-legged on a mountain outcrop, which Prokopiev would recognize many years later in reality as the pine forest of Molika. 'Excuse me –,' Prokopiev said to him in his dream, but not only did the man not turn around but indeed didn't notice him at all and kept on muttering something rhythmic to himself. Prokopiev tried to understand what the man was saying, but he could only make out a few rambling words that all contained the 'sh' sound: 'Kushli... shavi... ashogl... kishku...'. It was as if the old man was sending the words to the mountain and they were coming back as echoes.

* * *

A little earlier or later than that, Prokopiev began playing rock and roll. At the black Petrof piano at home he switched from doing music lessons to writing 'hits', and soon he formed a band with boys from the neighbourhood called 'Hogar', 'The Vikings' or something like that, which played for dances at high schools and community halls. Later he left to study in Belgrade and enrolled in comparative or 'world' literature.

In his first year he sat all his exams, got good marks, and also played evergreens at the Topčiderski Štimung nightclub, where the loose ladies greeted him with miaows. He rented a room from the Galić family in Proletarian Brigades Street, directly opposite the Nikola Tesla Museum. The Galićs had an old but excellently preserved piano, and their son Vlada and his friends from the final year of high school used to gather in the flat. Prokopiev and Vlada struck up a fond friendship after their very first meeting. Two of Vlada's school friends were also musically inclined, and later they were joined by a dark-skinned boy from the block of flats next door, who would be the drummer. And so, in the cellar of the block of flats, they set up a band and called it 'Zvuk Ulice' (Sound of the Street). They played instruments borrowed from unmusical children from rich families; Prokopiev remembers the Farfisa organs he was allowed to use for the first few gigs (at high schools and community halls, of course). They soon realized it was no good just having amplifiers but no instruments of their own. So every weekend they carted Western-bought jeans, old lamps, the odd sideboard, budgerigars and cracked amphoras to sell at the flea market in nearby Zemun. Afterwards they spent half the proceeds buying thank-you shirts and dresses for their zealous fans who had given them a hand, and they saved the other half in a rhinoceros-shaped piggy bank to buy new instruments with.

At that time, probably because when you play rock you let your rebellious side hang out off-stage as well, Prokopiev 'caused an affront' at university by squirting a water pistol at an assistant lecturer – later Serbia-Montenegro's ambassador to a major European country. He was on the verge of being expelled, but luckily old Professor Nestor only gave him a good scolding and let him stay on at university. There was a repeat performance of the same scenario ten years later, now back in Prokopiev's home city, where he was employed at the state radio station. The rock virus still raged inside him, so with a few other un-dead rock rebels he formed the band 'Usta na Usta' (Mouth to Mouth). They carried the day at a large rock festival, recorded a few little hits and put out a cassette. But at work Prokopiev received a pink slip for 'anarcho-liberalist deviations' or some equally absurd label. The tinpot Goebbels who had him sacked, the director of the radio station, was just another brick in the socialist-realist wall waiting to be toppled by angry crowds a few years later. But that is a story for another time.

* * *

But let us return to Belgrade and Prokopiev's days with 'The Sound of the Street': the band moved from practicing in the cellar to the spacious, white hall of the Student Cultural Centre. Some other guys were playing there too, whacky sorts, but young writers and artists also used to drop in, and after gigs Prokopiev would stay on until morning and discuss the revolution in the spirit, style and packaging of culture that the times called for. It was then that he began to publish work in Yugoslav literary magazines – poems in prose, prose in verse, impressions, and expressions. One of his fellow young writers of that time would later note: "Prokopiev and I first met in the long-past seventies in the tiny editorial office of the literary journal *Književna reč (Literary Word)*, back in its heroic days, in that brave age of creative and intellectual initiative. But that is a different story, and it wouldn't be right for me to harp on about it because I'm sure Prokopiev would get angry."

One thing was for sure: although Prokopiev had not been practicing his ping-pong for a long time, he began once more to draw energy from literature, to rev himself up and get high on it, like he used to in his high-school evenings in the park. In terms of getting high... yes, people smoked grass at the parties. The marijuana movement struck root among all the rock'n'rollers and some of the aspirants to the title of 'writer'. Moist little joints were passed around, with sleepy movements, from mouth to mouth. One of Prokopiev's muses – herself an aspiring writer, Allen Ginsberg's girlfriend, a globetrotter from India to Paris and three times married – to a Jew, a Buddhist and an Animist – used to go with him from Belgrade's *Golden Parrot* bar to her flat on the other side of the street for a joint together, often in the company of a handful of other folk, their eyes open but dreamy. They felt cosy together, but they didn't quite realize who was who, or from where they came.

* * *

Towards the end of this almost nine-year hot-cold stay in Belgrade, the incident with Mr Anonymous occurred.

Much later, after a quarter of a century had passed, Prokopiev found out that Anonymous had been causing trouble for him again. During one of the Novel of the Year competitions, where one of his books was 'in the running', the fellow sent an anonymous email to all the members of the judging panel and, in severe and insulting language, proceeded to blacken his name and brand him as a troublesome personality.

Prokopiev's reaction was immediate: he wanted to get hold of one of those accursed emails straight away and look into the affair again – there could be some characteristic trait, for example Anonymous might have particular quirks in punctuation and spelling... but, as usual, just as he set about dealing with the problem in earnest, he felt a strange lethargy in his body, and all the scary images from distant 1980 in Belgrade, from his first traumatic experience with Anonymous (mistakenly called 'memories' by some), began to gush forth.

'There's a man on the phone for you,' his flatmate Budo called out from the hall: 'He didn't say his name.'

Prokopiev shared a flat in Gračanička Street, in the centre of Belgrade, with Budo and Dobrica. Dobrica was a representative of a large food company and had the biggest space – two connected rooms with a balcony – while he and Budo had one room each, which nevertheless were large and had ceilings high enough to look like apartments in their own right.

'Yes?'

'Is that Prokopiev?'

'Speaking. Sorry, who is this?'

' '
...

'May I ask where you're calling from?'

'The Ministry of the Interior.'

For a few moments, neither of them spoke. Prokopiev was stunned and in the grip of the thought: 'They've found me. I'm done for!' The man at the other end was waiting (we may assume – sadistically) to see how he would react. Prokopiev's fear was entirely justified because he had not reported to the local police to register his place of residence, as one was required to. The first months after Tito's death had passed, and the city felt as if it was under invisible but constant surveillance. There were hidden informants all over the place: at the local-community offices, among the university's administrative staff, and perhaps even among the eavesdropping waiters. Even when, once a month, he would send a parcel of dirty washing home to Skopje, the man at the counter, who had previously greeted him with cheerful chatter, was now sullen as he processed the parcel.

'Look, what's this about?' Prokopiev asked the caller.

Around that time, independent of the general air of anxiety following Tito's death, he became fascinated to distraction with astrology. While a barrage of articles glorifying the life and work of the unique, 'international leader' filled the daily press, Prokopiev devoured dream books, astrological manuals and daily horoscopes. Exactly during that time, several months earlier, he had entered his first period of Saturn, which, according to astrological logic, marks the beginning of the first dangerous ordeals in life. Now, at the height of his fear, he arrived at the thought that this was happening to him because of bad old Saturn.

'I can't tell you now. You'll understand everything when we meet.'

'Meet? Where?'

'Be in Students' Park, at the monument to Josif Pančić, the Botanist, tomorrow afternoon at 12.30.'

'But... I don't know who you are.'

'What counts is that I know who you are! Till tomorrow at 12.30.'

Prokopiev tossed and turned in bed that night, imagining that the next day at that time he definitely would not be in the flat but shut away in some nameless interrogation cell, at the mercy of his judges. He wouldn't be able to see the faces of the prosecutor (Anonymous) or the jury members because a spotlight would be shining in his eyes, and this would certainly make him look even paler and paltrier in the eyes of Mr Anonymous in the dark. Anonymous's voice, just as threatening as over the phone but much louder, would speak to him sternly in Serbian: 'Comrade Prokopiev, to your feet! Do you have anything to say in connection with the investigations conducted to date and the face-to-face meeting with the witnesses?'

'I have nothing more to say than what I said during the... questioning. I would only ask to be forgiven for not telling the truth about the flat in Gračanička Street – for not registering my place of residence... When I was confronted with all the witnesses, I realized... I really ought to have stuck to the rules, especially because our country is in such a sensitive phase... I wouldn't want to be mistaken for an internal enemy because I have never been, nor will I ever be.'

It was no use. Now his sentence rang out:

It follows from the information presented that Comrade Aleksandar Prokopiev, a postgraduate student at the Faculty of Arts at the University of Belgrade, became involved in activities hostile to the society and government of the Socialist Federal Republic of Yugoslavia during the summer months of 1980. As a Yugoslav citizen of legally culpable age he has thus betrayed his socialist homeland and violated his oath of loyalty to the President and Supreme Commander, Marshal Tito, and the people.

Therefore, due to the justified suspicion that he has committed a criminal act, he is to be incarcerated until further notice.

Signed: Anonymous
PROSECUTOR AND EXECUTOR

What a nightmarish scenario! Just imagine Prokopiev's fear, how little he had slept, and how many worst-case scenarios were weighing on his mind when he showed up in front of the Pančić monument the next day, fifteen minutes before the appointed time. What could the man do to him? What punishments were in store in for his inadmissible transgression?! How could he be so stupid as not to register his place of residence – and just after the death of Marshal Tito, of all times?! He fretted and fidgeted around the monument, gazed at the passers-by hurrying on their way and men with caps sitting on the benches, and after twenty minutes he even stopped one of them. The guy was wearing dark glasses and had a newspaper in his hand: 'Are you looking for me, perhaps?' 'I don't think so, no,' the man replied derisively, after sizing him up.

He waited a whole hour longer. No one came up to him. There was no sign of Anonymous from the Ministry of the Interior.

Feeling very small and petrified with fear, Prokopiev headed back to the flat. A fine summer rain began to fall in the streets of the Old Town, evaporating as soon as it touched the ground.

* * *

Despite all the everyday joys that Prokopiev sometimes thinks up just in order to survive, he is at other times assailed by a powerful feeling of being in exile in the very country he lives in. Normally the remedy for this condition is travel. Travelling enlivens the spirit but also ruins your teeth, be it because of all the changes in food, water, or the microclimate – so a denture was the first artificial aid he had to get accustomed to. And although Prokopiev has to go to the dentist after every trip, he hasn't lost one iota of his enthusiasm for peregrination – both beyond the borders of his home country and within them. Sometimes just a few kilometres are enough to seclude him from the city, where being amidst a forest meadow cheers him up and where he can sit for hours watching a balding, old bird peck around in the grass. There, in a green notebook, he would note down the haiku:

Naked Mountain tall
A stark name, but misleading
– forest all around.

Prokopiev is firmly convinced that isolation in nature is the best medicine for his feeling of exile in society. But after two or three days of solitude he is hungry once again for the trivial pleasures of the human beehive, so he returns to the hair-splitting, hovels and architectural disasters of that city called Skopje.

* * *

For a time, Prokopiev was placed in an institution that was particularly animated on the inside but protected on the outside by high walls and padlocked gates, whose combination lock numbers were known only to a handful of warders in white. There he befriended the Man with the Third Eye, who, in contrast to the other three-eyed people, had his eye not in the middle of his forehead but on his chest, so that it was hidden beneath his pyjamas and thus invisible to others, even for the Chief Warder in white, who noted down the nouns, pronouns, adjectives and verbs that each of the inmates spoke every day in a thick logbook. When in front of him, the Man with the Third Eye was completely stupefied and muttered disconnected syllables and absurd words like 'frooteh', 'atrochy', 'gnederit' or 'shadabo'. The Chief Warder pedantically noted down all these vocal unravellings in his book, pensively shaking his head, but Prokopiev was convinced the Man with the Third Eye was just pretending to be feeble-minded, although he had never admitted it, so as to have a bit of fun with the warders. 'That will keep him nicely barking up the wrong tree for a while,' Prokopiev whispered to encourage him to keep on concealing the truth, but the Man with the Third Eye glanced at him in astonishment and replied: 'Choo-choo, quack-quack.' Prokopiev began to learn that emptiness is nothing terrible, impurity doesn't mean smut, and that regulations are not made for settling disputes but so that humanity has something more to laugh about. He did his best to see all the goings-on in the institution as scenes from a poorly written drama. In other words, that that world only exists here, on the stage, in the present tense; its duration is limited, and when the show is over the actors take a bow, the curtain falls, and the viewer, or rather Prokopiev, goes to bed. In a case like this, sleep can be one path home. And Prokopiev slept long and deep.

Once he happened to dream of the Man with the Third Eye, whom people in his dream called 'Teacher Brahmaputra'. He looked very much like the old man in the purple-red tunic from his earlier dream, but now he was much younger. The Man with the Third Eye, or Teacher Brahmaputra, now spoke clearly and comprehensively (which did not surprise Prokopiev at all) and was dressed in an orange tracksuit. He was sitting in the first row of the empty grandstand of Skopje's main stadium and cheering on the characters in the dream to keep riding their bicycles around the circular track. Prokopiev, who was riding a battered old bicycle that screeched with every turn of the pedals, was totally indisposed and bathed in sweat: 'I can't go on. I have so much concentrated black in me,' he complained to Teacher Brahmaputra, who just smiled from the grandstand: 'Look closer and you'll see an encouraging light within, behind the clouds. Keep pedalling, keep going. You can do it!'

* * *

It was probably back then, when he would submerge in those periods rich in loose, floating thoughts, between reality and dreams, and emerge from them again, that Prokopiev became convinced that there is a more or less effective way of cleansing oneself of the negative vibrations of chaotic surroundings and of one's own demons: to keep writing. A way of bridging all the cracks, pitfalls and precipices that make can life a misery. He had already had several small successes in literature, as mentioned earlier, but it became increasingly clear to him that he could do a lot more. And since that realization, fifteen books with his name on them have come out, imagine, and life goes on. No applause, please, because not all paths lead somewhere, and there are dead ends and sometimes you turn in circles, but that is not in vain, as Teacher Brahmaputra told us. What's important is that there's movement. I move, you move, everything moves, yes, yes, yes...

* * *

One of the luminaries of the domestic literary pantheon – an academic with the 'my word is final' mindset and other delusions of grandeur – declared today's literature to be 'a heap of empty-headed extravagancies'. Prokopiev, who engaged in verbal polemics with the same ardour and imprudence as he did in the neighbourhood scrimmages of boyhood, which he used to come away from with a bump on his head or a broken nose, now felt the blood rush to his face again, and he replied with a booming voice: 'You've obviously given up reading.' 'What rot!' the academic shouted back. Having always had problems with authority figures and people in uniform, as we've seen, Prokopiev grimaced and demonstratively stormed out of the room.

As defensible as this display and swagger may be, Prokopiev knows that the truth about writing and reading today is a multifaceted thing. Just as rock irreversibly melted down into soppy pop, film into vacuous Hollywood extravaganzas and graphic art into installations, so literature has begun to be identified with hyped bestsellers à la Paulo Coelho, Og Mandino and Dan Brown (at least among 'the broad reading public'). Faced with the ever-greedy worm of consumerism, the majority of creatives accept being partially blinded rather than going hungry. Prokopiev encounters ever more blinkered contemporaries like this – running in the dark and imagining their big breakthrough have made them forget that enchantment doesn't come out of thin air. A good ten years earlier, at the height of internet fever, his astrologist-friend Simoen told him that the stratification of interests and associations is inevitable and will lead to the creation of new circles and special-interest groups, where kindred spirits will communicate securely, almost secretively. Prokopiev is involved in one such group today. The other members are from all over the world, but it feels as if they are neighbours and live in the same street. And all of them believe, or almost believe, that fairy tales are still possible today: With a few minor or major adaptations, of course.

THE TRANSLATOR

WILL FIRTH was born in 1965 in Newcastle, Australia. He studied German and Slavic languages in Canberra, Zagreb and Moscow. Since 1991 he has been living in Berlin, Germany, where he works as a freelance translator of literature and the humanities. He translates from Russian, Macedonian, and all variants of Serbo-Croat. His website is www.willfirth.de.

THE AUTHOR

ALEKSANDAR PROKOPIEV (Macedonian: Александар Прокопиев), born in 1953 in Skopje, is a Macedonian writer, essayist and a former member of one of the most popular bands in ex-Yugoslavia (*Idoli*). He has a Ph.D. in Comparative Literature and currently works at the Institute of Literature at the Ss. Cyril and Methodius University of Skopje.

Throught his career, Prokopiev has worked on several domestic and foreign magazines, and was a member of the editorial board of *Orient Express* (Oxford, UK) and *World Haiku* (Kyoto, Japan). He has written several screenplays for film, theatre, TV shows, radio dramas and comic books. His works have been translated into English, French, Italian, Japanese, Russian, Polish, Hungarian, Czech and Slovak, among others.

Prokopiev is the author of several short story collectons: *The Young Master of the Game* (1983), *Sailing South* (1986), *A Sermon on the Snake* (1992), *Ars amater-ia* (1998), *The Man With Four Watches* (2003) and *Homunculus* (2011, winner of the 'Balkanika Award' for best book of the year). He has also published two collections of essays: *Was Callimachus a Post-Modernist?* (1994) and *Fairytale on the road* (1996); one collection of Haiku poems *Image which rolls* (1998); a published diary, *Anti-instructions for personal use* (2000) and the novel, *Pepper* (2007).